THIS BOOK
BELONGS
TO:

ID

NAME: _____

AGE: _____

SIGNATURE: _____

TOP THREE BISCUITS

1. _____
2. _____
3. _____

The Accidental Diary of **B.U.G.**

SISTER ACT

Jen Carney

PUFFIN

PUFFIN BOOKS

UK | USA | Canada | Ireland | Australia
India | New Zealand | South Africa

Puffin Books is part of the Penguin Random House group of companies
whose addresses can be found at global.penguinrandomhouse.com.

www.penguin.co.uk
www.puffin.co.uk
www.ladybird.co.uk

First published 2022
001

Text and illustrations copyright © Jen Carney, 2022

The moral right of the author/illustrator has been asserted

Text design by Janene Spencer
Printed in Great Britain by Clays Ltd, Elcograf S.p.A.

The authorized representative in the EEA is Penguin Random House Ireland,
Morrison Chambers, 32 Nassau Street, Dublin D02 YH68

A CIP catalogue record for this book is available from the British Library

ISBN: 978-0-241-45549-4

All correspondence to:
Puffin Books
Penguin Random House Children's
One Embassy Gardens, 8 Viaduct Gardens, London SW11 7BW

For beautiful Val, who believed in me
right from the start

FIRST THINGS FIRST

Hello! My name's Billie and I'm under my bedcovers about to start writing my third 'accidental' diary. Now it's your turn . . .

WHO ARE YOU?

A CHILD

A GROWN-UP

AN ALIEN

AND WHAT ARE YOU UP TO?

Hmspar mi doily-blap!

Err . . . reading this book . . .

Checking if this book is suitable reading material for my children.

Just as I thought! Hi! It's awesome to see you here. Please accept this free gift in recognition of your excellent book choice and let's get going!

Please skip ahead to section TTVx² on page 244.

✗ VOUCHER FOR MEALTIME ✗

This not-at-all-fake voucher allows me _____ (insert your name here)
to leave at least half of my_____ (insert word here)
by order of Billie Upton Green ☺

EXCITING NEWS

I found out some LIFE—CHANGING news on Friday
night. I was so desperate to share it with Class
Five today that I couldn't wait for show-and-
tell. LITERALLY. I just blurted it out at morning
registration.

Thankfully, Mrs Patterson wasn't in one of her
Monday-morning 'no yelling' grumps. 'Wow!' she
exclaimed. 'That's wonderful news.'

She even asked if anyone had any questions or
comments. Every single one of my classmates

flung an arm into the air. I'd like to say this was because they were EXTREMELY interested and dead pleased for me, but I suspect it was actually because they'd spotted the perfect opportunity to delay morning spellings.

Unfortunately, at moments like this, Mrs Patterson refuses to acknowledge anyone waving their arms around like a demented octopus. So, although I was desperate to hear what my #BBF, Dale Redman, had to say, Patrick North was the first person given the opportunity to congratulate me. Which he didn't.

#BEST BOY FRIEND

'Which of your mums is pregnant?' he asked.

Ignoring Patrick's sly smirk, I explained how neither of them is, but that my birth mother, Wendy, has had a baby, and that my mums will soon be ADOPTING her — just as they adopted me ten years ago.

My classmates already know about me being adopted and having two mums, so that wasn't NEWS at all. It was definitely an example of what Mrs Patterson would call 'OLDS'.

My #BFF, Layla Dixon, got picked next. She was THRILLED she could talk about my news in public. Apart from my great-nan, she's the only other person Mums had let me phone to WHOOP with over the weekend.

'I can't wait to meet her, Billie,' she said. 'I wonder if she'll look like you.'

I wonder that too. Layla's baby sister, Neela, is the absolute SPITS of her. I hope mine looks like me. Well, she and Neela are destined to become #BFFs, so it'll be awesome if our mini-mes look exactly like us just ten years behind.

Elliot Quinn was next. After saying 'Hongera!' which, FYI, means 'congratulations' in Swahili, he asked how old my new sister is.

I told him she's two months old. According to Elliot, that's the same as 8.7 weeks, which is the same as 1,460 hours, which is the same as 87,600 minutes. Elliot, as you can tell, is something of a MASTERMIND.

My final question came from Janey McVey. In case you don't know, she's been a complete **MEANIE—PANTS** to me in the past. 'Why is your sister not living with you **right now**?' she asked, raising one eyebrow as though she suspected I was sharing fake news. 'What is she waiting for?'

'Oh, Janey,' I replied, rolling my eyes so she didn't know that's what I've been wondering too. 'That's how things work when you adopt a baby; you don't just pick them up in a carrier bag and take them home like they're a bag of carrots from Aldi. It takes time.'

MADAM, YOU FORGOT YOUR BABY!

Mrs Patterson said it was time for our spellings challenge after that. I stopped myself wondering what exactly is causing the hold-up on my sister's arrival by trying to get my head around the difference between 'tion' and 'sion', and when I should use them. I came to the conclusion (well, actually, the conclu-shun) that 'shun' would do nicely for both, and used most of spellings time to draft a letter to my pen pal.

Dear prime minister,

As I've menshuned a cupple of times before, it's my ambi-shun to come up with a new dic-shun-ary that gives solu-shuns to stupidness in spelling so I don't have too many correc-shuns to do every day. It wud be mega splendid if all words cud be spelled eggzacly the way they sownd. As you can see, it will mayk reeding very eezy.

I hope to hear from you reelly soon.
Billie Upton Green (your pen pal who you rote to about biskits a fyew weeks bak)

PS Pleez cud you add 'thranimal' to the dik-shun-ary?

GIRAFLAMINGOAT
(MY LATEST THRANIMAL
INVENTION)

WHAT'S THE HOLD-UP?

MY MUMS:
SARAH AND KATIE

According to Mums, the reason my sister hasn't been delivered to us yet is because an ASSESSMENT has to be done to make sure we are 100% the best FOREVER FAMILY for her.

Who could possibly think any other family than ours would be a better FOREVER one for **MY SISTER**? I've no idea. Mums said it's something to do with rulers and red Sellotape. Although I

could be mistaken. I stopped listening as soon as I heard the word ASSESSMENT . . .

Mrs Patterson sometimes uses the word ASSESSMENT when she means TEST . . .

Like today, she said we were having an ASSESSMENT to check we were all on the right level of reading books, and it didn't go well for me. I'm not the best at tests. I often run out of time, or get distracted by inventing games or by the fact that my pencil needs sharpening again.

MY CURRENT PENCIL

What if the adoption ASSESSMENT includes a timed element where we have to think of ten reasons the baby should live with us in less than a minute? I'm sweating just thinking about it. Or what if I have to prove I can change a nappy? Dolls' bums covered in chocolate spread are easy, but I've never dealt

with a real-live baby with actual POOP in its bottom before.

What if I have to write an essay outlining everything I know about keeping babies safe? I can only think of three things: don't let them drink poison, never throw them down stairs, and keep them away from hungry sharks. There must be others.

Sorry to rush off, but I'm getting myself in such a state I'm going to have to nip downstairs to ask Mums more about this (and see if they're sneakily gobbling the bag of jelly babies I spotted earlier).

YELLOW NAILS

OK, I know a bit more now so I'm feeling
less panicky, and my stomach's
stopped rumbling . . .

Apparently the ASSESSMENT has already started!
A social worker called Margaret Mulvaney has
been chatting to Mums about our family and
whether we can cope with another child. Maybe
she heard about Mum K leaving Mr Paws tied up
outside school the other day. You probably can't
do that with babies.

Mums said this Margaret Mulvaney wants to have a few meetings with ME too! They told me I shouldn't panic because all I have to do is answer her questions honestly. I'm not sure whether WHITE LIES will be allowed, so apart from worrying about her turning up in a brown vest with pale-pink roses all over it and asking me, 'Do you like my top?' I'm quite looking forward to it.

I only know one other Margaret — the woman who works in the pie shop near Granny P's house. She has yellow fingernails and browny-yellowy teeth and she calls everyone 'pet'. I know not all Margarets will be like this, but that's what I'm imagining at the moment.

PS You know how when someone has a baby they can't look after for one reason or another, a foster family looks after them for a little while before they're adopted? Well, you'll never guess the name of the family looking after my sister until our ASSESSMENT has finished: **THE BOURBONS!** I can't wait to meet them. They sound delicious.

DANIEL

We have a new Friday teacher!

Mr Dilbert, who was called a 'supply' teacher
(which, FYI, is what you call old men who blow
their noses on small tablecloths and think an hour
of reading can be classed as Golden Time) has
been replaced by a fresh-smelling, drama-loving
smartboard expert called Mr Castle.

I suspected he was MY KIND OF PERSON straight
after assembly when, instead of making us

complete yesterday's corrections, he pulled a
~~youcalailee~~ ~~youcalaley~~ tiny guitar out of his
backpack and taught us a silly song. Singing
about 'Brenda Stowing whose hobby is throwing'
being in love with 'Tall Paul who can't catch
a ball' was an EXCELLENT start to the weekend
(which is basically what Friday is).

Next, he fired up the smartboard. Unlike Mrs
Patterson, he didn't encounter a single technical
difficulty AND he got the
volume button to go past
three, so we were
mesmerized even before
he loaded a file called
TOP SECRET.

It contained a slideshow of HILARIOUS photos,
which he whizzed through while telling us tons of
PRIVATE information about himself including, NO
WORD OF A LIE, his actual first name (Daniel).

ABOUT ME — DANIEL CASTLE

HOBBIES

BEST
FRIEND

FAVOURITE
FOODS

Blimey. The most private, unschooly thing I know
about Mrs Patterson is that she buys her

cardigans in the ASDA
sale (and I only know
this because Grandma
Jude often looks like her
clothes twin).

He's such a chatterbox; it was morning break
before we knew it. I know! #BestMorningEver
or what?

After break, Mr Castle stressed how important it

was that no one felt shy about asking questions or getting things wrong on Fridays, as that's the best way to learn. So, when he said he'd like to learn our names, I immediately

NO IDEA IS A BAD IDEA!

raised my hand to suggest we play Murder in the Dark (and SCREAM our names if we were killed). He thanked me for my idea but said he had a better one.

He didn't.

His idea was for us to write down our FULL NAMES and see how many other words we could make from them while he tiptoed around the classroom looking over our shoulders and saying hello. Grrr. It was basically a spelling challenge.

Anyway . . . I wrote BELINDA UPTON GREEN at the top of my paper and beneath it wrote:

a

bad

dog

burped

When Mr Castle came behind me, he said, 'Well done, BELINDA. I can think of a lot more than four words, though. What about "BUG" for example? That's staring me right in the face!'

Everyone looked round and gasped before Dale treated Mr Castle to the story of how NO ONE is allowed to call me 'Bug' without my permission, and how I like to be called Billie, not Belinda. Mr Castle said he understood as he prefers Dan

to Daniel. He wouldn't tell us his middle name,
so I'm guessing it's something embarrassing like
Underpants.

To be fair, that was
the only blip in an
otherwise amazing day
because after dinner
Mr Daniel (Underpants)
Castle told us something even more EXCITING
than his name.

Hang on a sec . . .

THIS WEEK'S SPELLINGS

SORRY
~~MUSICUL~~ musical
ABOUT
DRAMA
THIS
~~ORDISHUN~~ audition
~~INTERUPSHUN~~
           interruption

THANKS, MUM.

Don't worry. I haven't lost the plot. Let me explain what **THAT** was all about.

If I hear movement outside my bedroom door late at night and I don't have enough time to turn off my torch and fake that I'm sleeping, I sometimes have to flip to a new page and pretend I'm engrossed in learning spellings. There are three reasons for this:

1. My mums think this book is a SPELLINGS jotter.

Spellings Jotter

2. I have no wish for them to find out that, as with the

last such notebooks they gifted me, I've 'accidentally' repurposed it into a much more interesting STAY—AWAKE DOODLE DIARY.

3. Pretending I'm practising spellings never results in a 'you should be asleep' lecture. The worst I have to put up with is having my (usually fake) spellings corrected.

Anyway, now Mum's gone, let me get back to Mr Castle's exciting announcement . . .

He's setting up an after-school DRAMA CLUB, and anyone who attends will be involved in putting on the official WORLD PREMIERE of a brand-new ~~musicul~~ musical play.

If this afternoon's 'Taste of Drama' Golden Time is anything to go by, I'm signing up for sure.

We basically played a bunch of silly games for an hour — including my new favourite: **Answer the Question Before**. It's a bit difficult to explain, but I'll try my best as you'll 100% want to try it on your friends (and frenemies):

1. You ask someone a question that they DO NOT answer.

2. You ask them a second question. Their job is to give their answer to the first.

3. You ask a third question. Now they give their answer to the second.

For example:

ME: What did you have for pudding
          at dinner?

PATRICK: (no answer)

ME: What do you wipe your bottom with
          after you've done a poo?

PATRICK: Ice cream. (HA! See how that's the answer to question one?)

ME: What's our head teacher called?

PATRICK: Toilet roll. (The answer to the second question!)

ME: Who would you like to kiss before you leave school today?

PATRICK: Mr Epping.

(HA HA HA!)

As I found out, if you think about your questions carefully, it can be hilarious. EVERYONE (apart from Patrick) was in stitches.

Anyway, at home time, Mr Castle declared he'd be **honoured** if everyone in Class Five joined his 'Drama Crew', but I'm pretty sure he looked directly at **me** when he mentioned he'd witnessed some MAIN-PART POTENTIAL!

You know what? Despite his sneaky spelling challenge, I'm seriously considering DUC for the vacancy on my 'favourites' list, which has been up for grabs since its last occupant (she who shall not be named) left our school abruptly.

FAVOURITES

BISCUIT: custard cream

COLOUR: indigo (especially indigo galaxy patterns)

FRIEND: Layla (girl), Dale (boy)

PLANET: Uranus (hee hee)

TEACHER: ~~Mrs~~ Sharvane

MEAL: ketchup (with chips)

OBJECT: metal detector (100%)

DRINK: FROOT GOOP

MUM: Katrah!

NEW SISTER

You're NOT going to believe what I found out when I went to visit Great-Nan at her special home this afternoon!

I knew something was on her mind as soon as we got there.

For one, she wasn't sitting in the max-volume television room holding hands with her special-home man friend, Barmy Raymond.

For two, she forgot to sing 'Let It Go!' when I trumped extra loudly on walking into her bedroom.

And, for three, her glasses were on upside down.

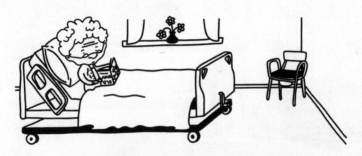

Mums didn't look too concerned, so I made myself semi-comfortable while they wiped toothpaste smears off her cardigan and turned her magazine the right way round.

'I've got some news,' said Great-Nan when Mums had stopped faffing about why she didn't have her false teeth in.

Great-Nan's 'news' isn't often terribly earth-shattering. I was fully expecting her to inform us she'd had her hair shampooed, or that her friend Nettie has sprouted another chin hair. So when she said she'd received a letter from her sister — **a sister she didn't even know she had** — I almost fell off my commode.

LIKE A GROWN-UP POTTY

As Great-Nan gets stuff a bit jumbled sometimes, Mums thought she was making it up. 'Oh, Nan!' said Mum S, reaching for Great-Nan's wrinkly hand. 'You're confused. It's Billie who's getting a new sister, remember?'

'I know that, dear,' replied Great-Nan, winking at me. 'I've not completely lost my marbles yet.'

Reaching into her handbag, she pulled out an envelope. 'Her name's Kathleen,' she stated, handing it to Mum.

Mum read the letter aloud. It was quite long and confusing, but what it boiled down to was this:

1. This Kathleen is seventy years old. She's lived in the same house by a rather splendid-sounding

beach all her life. She grew up as an only child and her parents died over twenty years ago.

2. A few months ago, her grandson had been rooting about in her loft, trying to find out more about his ~~ansestors~~ ~~ansessters~~ old relatives so he could make a family tree, when he discovered some SECRET papers.

3. One of the SECRET papers revealed that Kathleen's mother had given birth to a SECRET baby twelve years before Kathleen was born.

4. Another proved the SECRET baby had been adopted when it was two days old.

5. Kathleen was flabbergasted.

6. Kathleen's family hired some kind of people-finding detective who discovered the SECRETLY adopted baby was none other than . . .
Yep, you guessed it,
MY GREAT-NAN!

So, in a nutshell, my eighty-two-and-three-quarter-year-old great-nan has just found out:

1. She was adopted when she was a baby —
JUST LIKE ME!
2. She has a little sister she's never met —
JUST LIKE ME!

I know! It's no wonder we've always got on so well.

It was fascinating to learn how similar I am to my great-nan, but what I couldn't understand was the MASSIVELY DIFFERENT THING — why on earth had it all been kept such a SECRET?

Mum S explained how, for one reason or another, families often kept adoptions 'hush-hush' in the old days. I said I was totally glad I'd been born in the new days. Well, I've known forever whose front bottom I popped out of. It's no big deal, but I'm glad I know.

Great-Nan didn't seem at all cross with her dead parents for never telling her the truth about her adoption. In fact, she said something uber-wise that I'm 100% going to remember ALL MY LIFE — like next time I wish I could still squeeze my feet into my size-three rainbow laces, or when Mrs Patterson asks to hear me read when she's got coffee breath.

THERE'S NO POINT DWELLING ON THINGS YOU CAN'T CHANGE.

Anyway . . . Kathleen has asked Great-Nan if she wants to meet up. I said she ABSOLUTELY should, and that as a bit of an expert on having a new sister I've not met yet, I'd certainly accompany her to Something-by-the-Sea.

Unfortunately, Great-Nan wasn't awfully keen on the idea. She said it was because she and Barmy Raymond have recently made plans to join the special home's karaoke club, which will take up a lot of their 'being awake' time, but I suspect she's actually nervous about needing the commode on a long journey. I suggested she write back, so Kathleen could be her pen pal — like the prime minister is mine. She said she'd think about it.

I've been thinking about it LOADS since we came home. If I'm going to meet my sister, it seems only right I should help Great-Nan to meet hers . . .

I'll get my thinking cap on.

BRIGHT STAR

Today I had my first **extremely important**
meeting with Mrs Margaret Mulvaney —
the social worker in charge of our adoption
ASSESSMENT.

Thankfully, she looked nothing like
the Margaret from the pie shop
near Granny P's, so I stopped
worrying about whether white
lies were acceptable and kicked
off the meeting with a bit of
honest Heart-Heating.

Heart-Heating, in case you don't know, is what
Mums call paying someone a compliment out
loud. They say it makes people go to bed smiling.
It definitely works because once Patrick North,
who is usually a huge annoying PEST, told me he
liked my handwriting. That made me feel a bit

better at bedtime when I was going through the events of my day, wondering why I'm the only girl in Class Five who's not got a pen licence yet.

So, quite honestly, I said, 'I like your front teeth, Margaret.'

Margaret laughed and told me no one had ever said that to her before, so I felt sure she'd remember the compliment at her bedtime.

'So, what do you think about the possibility of getting a new baby sister, Billie?' she asked, pulling a packet of Jaffa Cakes out of the wheelie suitcase she'd hauled into our house.

I wasn't fond of the way she said '**possibility**', but I didn't say so as I didn't want to ruin the **possibility** of being offered my second-favourite biscuit. Instead I told her how I'm mega excited and mentioned the tons of baby-care experience I have.

Margaret was so impressed she handed me the WHOLE PACKET of Jaffa Cakes and said, 'Help yourself.' (This nearly-having-a-new-sister business gets better every day!)

BISCUIT LAW 3

THE 'COMPLETELY DECONSTRUCT IT' CHARTER

Thou shalt endeavour to take it apart completely, saving the sweet disc of jelly till last.

While I taught Margaret how to correctly deconstruct a Jaffa Cake, which (solely for the purpose of education, you understand) involved eating three more biscuits each, she reached back into her suitcase. This time she pulled out a thick writing pad, a glue stick, three pieces of craft paper and . . . a tin of Quality Street!

'I wonder if you could use these things to make a picture of your family?' she said.

Smudging chocolate around paper to create lickable art didn't sound very meetingy. It did sound quite FABULOUS, though, so I nodded my head and waited for the fun to begin, wondering why Mums had never mentioned how delicious meetings can be.

Unfortunately, however, the chocolate tin contained nothing but a bunch of dried-up felt-tips. Don't you just hate it when that happens? It's an old-people's trick I should know by now. Granny P is the master of such storage. She has a sewing kit disguised as a Celebrations tin and a Heroes tub full of 2ps and 1ps.

When I'd got over my disappointment, I drew a quick sketch of our family. I rushed it a bit because I wanted to show Margaret my newest favourite thing to draw:  an any-way-up face. I figured it would totally showcase my **'thinking up marvellous ideas for babies'** skills.

'Look at this, Margaret,'
I said. 'If you turn the
paper upside down, it still
looks like a face, only a
sad one.'

Margaret agreed it was fascinating, but then
pointed to my family picture and asked me if
I could think of anything I'd like to add to it.
I patterned Mum K's jumper
with stripes and gave
myself a thought bubble.

Cocking her head to one side,
Margaret wrote something on her pad and then
asked me whether I'd like to add my new sister
into my picture. After a moment of panic, I
pointed at the faded yellow scribble in the corner
of the page. Between you and me, it had been
me testing a felt-tip that had been stored
without its lid, but Margaret wasn't to know.

'She's right there,' I said, wishing I'd not rushed. 'She's the wonderful bright star we're all dreaming of.'

Margaret laughed and said I was 'a clever one'. I'm not exactly sure whether she meant for the star idea or my speedy (whitish) lie but I thanked her all the same.

Next, to prove what a fabulous big sister I'm going to be, I made Margaret a paper aeroplane. Margaret forgot to say thank you, so I said, 'You're welcome!' to remind her. This prompted her to write TONS of notes. I couldn't quite see what they said because, for one, her handwriting was far too squiggly for me to read — I suspect she uses pen without having earned her pen licence. And, for two, she hides her work with her arm like Farida Banerjee during times-tables tests. But I expect it was something along the lines of: *Billie is incredibly grown-up, well* mannered and kind, and there's no doubt she'll be a wonderful role model for her sister. Deliver the baby ASAP.

Before she went home, Margaret asked if I had any questions for her. I enquired how she made her hair stripy and what her favourite ice-cream flavour was. The answers were: 'old age' and 'vanilla'.

I'd been worried before Margaret arrived, but I'm actually rather looking forward to our next meeting. She said she'd bring custard creams.

GAFF

We had our first Drama Crew session today. It was awesome. No one from Class Six came, so us Class Fivers finally got to do TOP CLASS ONLY stuff like sit on the red-cushioned benches and operate the music system.

First, to help the tiny Class Three kids stop being shy, Mr Castle let us play Wink Murder (also a perfect game for showcasing further main-part potential skills).

Next, we played a ~~kayotic~~ ~~cayotik~~ wild imagination game called Strike a Pose. Basically Mr Castle yelled an instruction, like *'Four people. You're carrying a million-pound piano up an escalator . . .*

GO!' Or 'Two people. One of you has split your pants walking into assembly . . . GO!' and we had ten seconds to get into groups of the right number and strike a silent(ish) pose of the situation he'd described.

It was funny (apart from when Janey McVey grabbed Layla and Dale for all the three-person situations, leaving me with Farida Banerjee and Patrick North).

After that, we played **Who Am I?** This involved us taking turns to do impressions. For my turn, I hid behind the hall door for a full minute. No one got who I was, but everyone agreed I'd done an excellent impersonation of a sister I've not met yet.

Dale's Who Am I? was the funniest, though. He looked scarily like Mr Epping. He borrowed Elliot's glasses, pushed them to the end of his nose, flattened his hair, scowled and yelled, 'Children, this is no laughing matter!'

Everyone ROARED with laughter, even Mr Castle . . . until we realized Mr Epping himself had chosen that exact moment to creep into the hall to see how Drama Club was going.

MR CASTLE, COULD I HAVE A QUIET WORD?

Mr Castle stopped whooping after that. He didn't prevent us doing a quiet(ish) shoe drum roll when he declared he was ready to announce the title of the WORLD PREMIERE we're going to perform, though.

It's called **CHIFFCHAFF'S NEW GAFF**. And, before you ask (as we did), 'gaff' is a slang word for home. It's a musical comedy, all the characters are birds, and the gist of the story is that little Chiffchaff, the main part, is searching for an adult bird who'll share their nest with them. Splendidly Mr Castle said each role is 'gender-fluid', which basically means that anyone can play any part.

Mr Castle has written the script **and** composed every song by himself and he's dead eager to get started, so main-part AUDITIONS are next week.

I already know what I want to be — Daredevil Dove. Not only does that part have the only full solo in the show, but, if the lines of its song are accurate, whoever gets to play it will definitely need to be rigged up with BUNGEE ROPES to look like they're flying.

DOIN' THE NOSEDIVE JIVE!

Layla fancies the part of Eggless — that's the silkie hen who ends up giving Chiffchaff a home. But she might change her mind once she's digested the script. I've noticed Fin (the puffin) has five pufflings who constantly follow it around begging for food — so she'd certainly be able to gain some expert tips from her mum if she landed that role.

Dale wants to be Ozzy the Ostrich, mainly because it gets to run fast through the audience and scoff jelly snakes on stage.

Janey McVey said she wants to be Chiffchaff — she would.

ATTENTION—SEEKER

PLAN A

I've set my GREAT-NAN-MEETING-HER-LONG-
LOST-SISTER plan into action.

Tonight, while Great-Nan's eyes were transfixed
on Barmy Raymond as he murdered 'Cry Boy
Jukebox' (my favourite-ever Zakk-O song) on
the special home's karaoke machine, I snuck to
her bedroom, copied Kathleen's address down
and, just now, I wrote this letter.

Dear Kathleen,

Hello. My name is Billie and I'm your long-lost sister's great-granddaughter.

Guess what! I'm adopted too! And I also have a sister I've not met yet. Can you believe it?!

My great-nan has quite shaky hands so she's not the best at writing. She's asked me to write to you to ask if you want to meet up. ~~I~~ We would love to come ~~for a jolly holiday~~ to Something-by-the-Sea.

Great-Nan is also not the best reader as her eyes have worked very hard over the past nearly eighty-three years. Please send your reply to me so I can read it to her.
Thank you.
Lots of love,
Billie Upton Green
PS I like biscuits.

PS Barmy Raymond comes out with some bonkers stuff. This evening he claimed he'd eaten a pencil for lunch, insisted a kangaroo lives in his bedroom and, most UNBELIEVABLE of all, told us his great-nephew, Cyril, composed 'Cry Boy Jukebox'. Ha! I mean, I don't know for sure about the pencil or the kangaroo, but, as Zakk-O's number-one fan, I can say with COMPLETE CONFIDENCE he writes his own material.

PPS My love for Zakk-O is purely based on his talent, not (as Mums say) because he's 'dishy' (by which they mean pleasant to look at; Zakk-O certainly doesn't resemble a dish).

STEALING MY THUNDER

Apart from Layla, Dale and Janey, I'd not told anyone else in Class Five about Great-Nan and how similar we are. So, when it got to show-and-tell time this afternoon, I shot my hand into the air. Unfortunately, six other people did too.

PATRICK   FARIDA   ME   CORAL   PERRY
                DALE   LAYLA

While Patrick North blabbered on about his mum's boyfriend's infected tongue piercing (gross), I ~~seruptishusly~~ ~~surupticiously~~ secretly attempted to persuade my remaining five competitors to let me go next — in case Mrs Patterson got into one of her impatient moods.

ONE SHOW-AND-TELL IS ENOUGH FOR TODAY. LET'S CHANT OUR SEVEN TIMES TABLE BEFORE THE BELL!

I convinced Layla, Dale and Coral easily. I was just trying to catch Perry Larkin's eye when Mrs Patterson said, 'Right, who'd like to go next?'

I raised my hand again. So did Farida and Perry. I may have huffed — slightly. BIG MISTAKE.

'Thank you for not exhaling loudly, Farida Banerjee,' gushed Mrs Patterson, giving me a stern glare. 'Would you like to go next?'

Farida (who jumps on every possible opportunity to use the word FAB to remind us that they're her initials) showed us forty-seven photos of YET

ANOTHER 'FAB-ulous' wedding she'd been to
(YAWN).

'Right,' bellowed Mrs Patterson (possibly to wake
everyone up) when Farida had finished, 'we've
got time for two more . . . if they're quick.'

I relaxed a bit then. Only me and Perry were
waiting. Or so I thought . . .
until I turned round and saw
Janey McVey with her left
index finger on her lips and
her right one pointing straight
at the ceiling.

I willed myself not to shout out — a rainbow
rule Mrs Patterson is always telling me I should
know backwards by now (which I do: **Class in
out shouting no!**) but I couldn't believe Janey
was trying to swoop in at the last minute.
'You've got to be kidding me!' I semi-yelled.

As you might be able to imagine, I didn't get chosen next. Perry did.

I scowled at Janey before listening to Perry's detailed account of how, at the weekend, he'd given his Barbie a makeover using a flamingo-patterned feather boa, nine pink Smarties, a length of pinkish wire and a glue gun.

Perry is obsessed with pink. His twin sister, Peace, on the other hand, hates it. It works out well for Perry, because every time Peace is gifted pink clothes or lipstick or anything, she donates them straight to him.

After Perry, Mrs P looked at me and Janey in turn. I held my breath (so I couldn't be accused of exhaling too loudly) while Janey sat so straight I thought she had a metre ruler stuck up her pinafore.

Everyone else kept swinging their heads back and forth, watching us as though we were competing in an intense table-tennis match.

'I think we'll see what Janey has to say,' said Mrs Patterson eventually.

ARGH!

'I was just going to say I think Billie should go next,' said Janey, fluttering her eyelashes. 'Because I know she's dying to tell everyone about how her great-nan's just found out she's got a sister she's never met. Whereas my news is just that my dad and his boyfriend, Benjamin, are thinking of moving house so they can live nearer to me.'

'Well, that's lovely, Janey,' replied Mrs Patterson, ignoring the fact that Painy McVey had COMPLETELY spoiled my moment, sneakily given her news AND pretended to be nice at the same time. 'Give yourself three team points for being considerate.'

Can you believe it?
And THREE team points?!
Janey is such a teacher's pet.

Mrs Patterson has only ever awarded more than two team points once before. That was when Elliot brought in a castle he'd made out of matchsticks (which, BTW, deserved a GOLD MEDAL, never mind three measly team points).

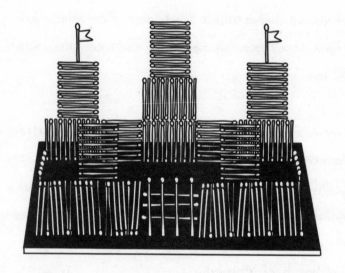

TOBY!

GUESS WHAT!!

I got a letter back from Kathleen-the-Seasider today. Well, TBCH, it was from someone called Toby who claims to be Kathleen's great-grandson. Like me, he was doing his elderly relative a huge favour *'saving her from hand ache'*. He sounds pretty cool.

Anyway, the upshot of the letter is that Kathleen desperately wants to come with Toby to see my great-nan *'so the long-lost sisters can meet before they die'*.

I wrote back immediately, giving this Toby directions to our house and informing him we've plenty of sleeping bags if they want to stay over. Although a trip to the beach would've been nice, I must admit this is a better plan. With her extra-trembly legs, Great-Nan might have struggled if we'd had to bunk on Kathleen's living-room floor. And I suppose it would've been quite a challenge transporting Great-Nan and all her equipment.

Now I just need to find a way to tell Mums about my AMAZING plan. And Great-Nan, I guess. Though maybe it'll be better if it's a GINORMOUS surprise? Ooooooh, I'm loving the sound of that.

BRIBERY

Janey McVey sucked up to Mr Castle BIG TIME at Drama Club this evening. She's mega desperate to be chosen to play Chiffchaff — mainly because she adores being the centre of attention.

MAIN PART

While the rest of us practised 'Boom! Boom! We've Got No Room!' (my favourite whole-cast number), she took Mr Castle to one side and told him all about how she starred in an advert about school uniforms a few weeks ago (so dull, BTW).

BOOM! BOOM! NO ROOM!

Then, immediately after Mr Castle reminded everyone that auditions are on Monday, she produced an ENORMOUS bar of chocolate from her book bag and gave him a delicious-looking chunk of it. Talk about trying to bribe your way into a part.

I, on the other hand, am going to rely solely on my talent to secure the role I want. I've actually just been going through the dove's audition piece with Mr Paws (quietly, of course — it's nearing Mums' bedtime). Mr Paws is not the best at delivering my cues, but he's excellent at making my bedroom stink like wild-bird poo, so I really got into character and I think I'm in with a good chance.

Plus, I conducted a quick poll earlier. If my facts are right, the only other person who'll be auditioning for Daredevil Dove on Monday is Daisy Muirhead. As Daisy's voice barely reaches a whisper when she has to speak in front of the class, I'm not overly concerned. But, to be sure, I've asked Mum if Layla can come over tomorrow so we can test each other on our lines. She said 'maybe', so I'm going to sleep with my fingers crossed to see if it works.

UNBIASED

IT WORKED! Layla came over and we spent AGES practising for our auditions.

First I was the judge while Layla sang 'Eggless's Lament' — a ~~meloncollie~~ ~~mellancolly~~ sad song where the silkie

hen describes how much it wants a baby to look after but can't lay eggs. Layla has a nice singing voice, but I think Peace Larkin might get that part because Peace and Perry's dad is the farmer who brings the eggs that hatch into chicks into reception class every year. Plus, Peace looks like this:

PEACE

SILKIE HEN

Then Layla judged my performance of 'The Nosedive Jive' — Daredevil Dove's jazzy song-and-dance number. The dance I've ~~coreograffed~~ ~~corryagraphed~~ created for my audition is AMAZING. I hop about from one leg to the other, flapping my arms wildly while I sing the first verse, nosedive towards the audience during the chorus, then fly around the barn gracefully at the end.

In our pretend version of auditions, despite Layla informing me I looked like a demented chicken trying to squeeze out an oversized egg, we both secured the parts we wanted. We even had the roles of Robin Redbreast, Confident Crow, Duddly Muck (the duck that gets all its words muddled up), the gammy-legged pigeon **and** Fin the Puffin added to our responsibilities because we were so UTTERLY TALENTED.

The only main roles we didn't get were:

- Ozzy the Ostrich (which we left open for Dale)
- Chiffchaff (we're realistic — that'll have to be someone diddly from Class Three) and
- the turkey (who, apart from the odd 'gobble, gobble' here and there, is more like a narrator, so should go to someone who can remember lines and speak loudly but can't act — like Farida).

IMHO Layla and I would make excellent and completely unbiased casting directors.

BRB . . .

SPELLING HOMEWORK

SPAG CHALLENGE

Using a range of punctuation, put the words **throughout**, **although**, **despite**, **however** and **nevertheless** into five interesting sentences.

Throughout is one of my spellings.

Look: although is one of my spellings.

Why is despite one of my spellings?

'Nevertheless is one of my spellings,' I said.

Blimey! One of my spellings is however.

Sorry about that short interruption. Mum swooped in to see why my torch was still on and the only thing I could think of was this weekend's **actual** spelling homework. I needn't have bothered. Mum wasn't remotely interested in inspecting my SPELLINGS jotter tonight. She just sat on my bed, put her arm round me and said, 'Is everything all right? You looked like you had the weight of the world on your shoulders at teatime.'

She doesn't miss a trick, Mum. I *have* had a bit of shoulder ache recently. It's not easy holding a torch, keeping a duvet off my face **AND** doodling in here. I couldn't admit to that (obvs). And I didn't want to talk about what I'd actually been thinking about at teatime, so I said I was anxious about my audition and nervous about my next adoption ASSESSMENT meeting with Margaret Mulvaney (neither of which were complete lies).

The actual truth is that I'd been wondering what Kathleen-the-Seasider will think of Great-Nan when she comes up for her sleepover. After we'd dropped Layla home, you see, we bobbed over to the special home. Great-Nan was on the commode when we arrived so we sat in the TV room with Raymond. Well, when Great-Nan eventually wobbled in to greet us, she apologized by saying, in a voice loud enough for the whole TV room to hear, 'Sorry to keep you waiting — I've been having a long poo!' Then, as if that wasn't funny enough, she added, 'As in it took ages to come out, not the shape of it!' I hope long-lost Kathleen isn't like Mrs Patterson — aka one of those serious old women who turn their noses up if anyone makes a joke about poo.

PS While Great-Nan was long-pooing, Barmy Raymond blabbered on about his too-perfect-to-be-real-sounding great-nephew, Cyril, so much that I decided to distract him by asking if he had any tips about auditioning. Once he told me that he was an actor in something called *His Day* (which I've never actually heard of, but I suspect it was made before TVs were in colour).

He did as it happens.

PEE BEFORE YOUR TURN.

They're a match made in heaven, those two.

EMERGENCY!

When I woke up this morning, I thought a
miniature bongo player had crept into my mouth
overnight to practise
drumming on my
lower left gum.

'You look like a
hamster that's
crammed too much food in one side of its

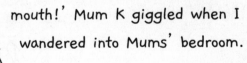

mouth!' Mum K giggled when I
wandered into Mums' bedroom.

'Oh dear, Billie,' said Mum S,
peering into my mouth when she
realized I was neither able nor willing to smile.
'That's quite some abscess.'

An abscess, in case you don't know (as I didn't),
is a HUGE, painful lump that meanly creeps its

way on to your gum in the night, wakes you up early and makes you cry. An abscess may or may not be caused by eating too many biscuits . . .

Mum K soaked a tissue in salty water and shoved it on my gum to help with the pain. It didn't. By 9 a.m., my face felt like it might explode, and I'd been sick twice.

I ended up being bundled into the car and rushed off to an EMERGENCY dentist miles away from home. I was in so much pain I didn't even whinge about missing out on the Sunday-morning special of *Saleema Selective: High-School Detective*. I did, however, spend most of the journey panicking I might have to have an INJECTION.

I shouldn't have worried. EMERGENCY dentists, it turns out, are AMAZING.

For one, they give you iPads to play on to calm you down.

AHHH!

OOOOH!

For two, they have access to magical cream. You don't feel a thing when they root around in your mouth — not even when they stick a needle into your gum.

MAGICAL STRAWBERRY-FLAVOURED STUFF!

And, for three, they tell your mum you deserve a SUBSTANTIAL present for being brave.

The dentist I saw was called Jerome. He was a right chatterbox. After he'd lessened my pain, we talked for ages, mostly about his teeth — one

of which was made of actual pure gold. I wished
I'd taken my metal detector with me. Actually
I might ask Mum if we can swap dentists
permanently. Jerome is loads more interesting
than our usual dentist (Ms Kelly) who can only
say three words: 'open', 'close' and 'spit'.

Just a minute . . .

SPOMEWORK

WORD INVENTIONS

Word invention	Definition
quinker	quick thinker
meacher	mean teacher
thranimal	three animals combined as one, e.g.

KOALANTIGER

Nentist	nice dentist
Rubbift	rubbish gift

Sorry (again). Mum's been in to see how I'm feeling. After she'd had a peek in my mouth, she commented on how 'creative' my spelling homework was. I panicked that she was ON TO ME until she gave me another word to add to my list: *braughter* — brave daughter!

Then, get this, I mentioned how my gum is still feeling a bit sensitive but that a biscuit and a mug of hot chocolate might help, and guess what she replied . . .

NO, IT'S TOO LATE FOR THAT, BUT YOU CAN HAVE A DAY OFF TOMORROW IF YOU'RE STILL FEELING POORLY.

Unbelievable! Mum is usually one of those parents who'd send you to school if your leg was hanging off. Trust it to be AUDITION DAY tomorrow. There's NO WAY I'm missing that.

GO ON, YOU'LL BE FINE.

PS In case you're wondering, my 'rubbift' was an electric toothbrush . . . I mean it's not too bad, but, between you and me, I'm a bit disappointed that being a braughter in the face of dental trauma (drauma?) was not considered iPad-worthy.

TERRIDAY

Today has been TERRIBLE.

The first sign of trouble was when I woke with gum ache again . . . at 5 a.m.

The second was when I said hi to Layla in the line and she asked me if I was sucking a gobstopper.

OOOH, CAN I HAVE ONE?

The third was when Mrs Patterson made me stay in at morning break to redo my SPAG worksheet — meaning I was the only Class Fiver not to attend Mr Castle's last-chance-saloon 'Audition Tips' workshop.

So unfair, BTW. I mean is this, or is this not, a list of seven verbs?

SPAG TASK 1
Write seven interesting verbs.

Bounce

Open

Obliterate

Burp

Inspect

Eat

Swim

Things went further downhill after break. My gum throbbed so much I couldn't speak properly. Not even to say something rude to Janey McVey when she came back into class BOASTING that Mr Castle had let her make his audition timetable. 'Don't worry, Billie,' she said. 'I didn't forget you. You're going FIRST.'

I wasn't particularly bothered about going first,

until Dale told me Janey had put herself last so Mr Castle wouldn't forget her performance when making his important casting decisions. Grrr.

The afternoon was even worse than the morning. Our school secretary, Miss Woods, called me to her office after dinner and told me Mum had dropped off some medicine for my toothache. I knew I should've kept quiet at breakfast. It looked VILE — all brown and gloopy. Miss Woods practically force-fed me a HUGE spoonful. It tasted of ~~lickrish liqriss~~ DISGUSTING.

It also made me tired. An hour later, I found myself being yelled at by Mrs Patterson for falling asleep. I blamed the evil medicine, but in reality being forced to work in TOTAL SILENCE to complete a comprehension about concrete probably hadn't helped.

I felt a bit more alert by home time, but as soon
as Mr Castle called me into the hall for my

audition I realized the medicine
also contained a memory-losing
substance. As well as talking like
I had a tangerine in my mouth,
I forgot loads of my lines and
almost all my dance moves.

THIS WILL
MAKE YOU:
· FALL ASLEEP IN
  BORING LESSONS
· FORGET
  AUDITION LINES

Oh well, as a wise woman once told me, **there's
no point dwelling on things you can't change**.
All I can do now is wait (and be thankful Daisy
Muirhead went home with a tummy ache at
afternoon break).

PEAR-SHAPED

I had my second ASSESSMENT meeting with
Margaret Mulvaney after tea today.

This time I was TOTALLY prepared. I'd drawn a
picture of myself carrying my nearly-here sister,
changed into my stripy black-and-white jumper
(to match Margaret's hair) and got out a plate
ready for our custard creams (my abscess has
vanished in case you were wondering).

Unfortunately, Margaret hadn't put as much
thought into our meeting as me. No biscuits
appeared at any time.

The first thing Margaret did was stare at our
fridge. 'WOW!' she exclaimed, her eyebrows
jumping to her fringe. 'Star of the Week, hey?
What did you get that for, Billie?'

That's when I noticed Mums had done a BIG clean. Not only had 'corned-beef island' been wiped off the enormous shiny world map pinned to our kitchen wall, all the lists, random letters from school and money-off coupons had disappeared from the fridge, leaving my certificate in full view.

Unfortunately, I'm yet to get the 'official' Star of the Week award for Class Five. Mainly because Mrs Patterson is picky.

TO GET STAR OF THE WEEK IN CLASS FIVE, ALL SEVEN RAINBOW RULES MUST BE FOLLOWED ALL WEEK.

I **may** have used Mum's laptop to expertly create the certificate Margaret was pointing to . . .

And been treated to a **'we're proud of you'**
takeaway and a late night the evening I produced
it . . .

Making it virtually impossible to come clean about
the certificate being a fake . . .

So I mumbled something about it being for
'helping people', hoping Margaret would move on
to conducting a nappy-changing test. No such
luck. She was E⟨TRA interested in **who** I'd
helped specifically and **how**.

All I could think of was how today, while
Mrs Patterson taught us about Roman numerals,
I helped Dale not fall asleep by inventing
Water-Bottle Bingo.*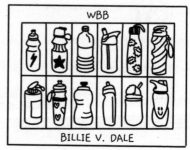
(Worked amazingly,
BTW.) I shuffled about
on my seat for a bit
and could feel my ears

*Water-Bottle Bingo rules are on page 234 if you want to try it!

turning pink. Then I suddenly remembered how I also helped my #BBF to speed-memorize the main Roman numerals when Mrs Patterson said she'd be keeping people in at playtime if they were struggling.

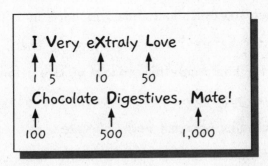

I Very eXtraly Love
↑ ↑ ↑ ↑
1 5 10 50
Chocolate Digestives, Mate!
↑ ↑ ↑
100 500 1,000

(C% proof that it's entirely possible to learn **AND** make up games at the same time.) So I told Margaret about that.

Margaret narrowed her eyes, tottered to the fridge to inspect the certificate more closely, then returned to the table, wrote something in her pad and commented on how 'imaginative' I am. I couldn't concentrate after that. I knew she knew I'd white-lied.

'Your mums have been telling me all about your great-nan,' she said, after a long silence. 'How are you feeling about that?'

I told her how glad I am my adoption has never been kept secret, and that I'm hopeful I'll meet my sister before I turn eighty-two. Then, as my white lie had made my mouth go dry, I went to fetch us both some juice. I poured it into wine glasses because Mum always uses posh things when we have visitors.

I wish I hadn't. They caused the meeting to go all pear-shaped. I let go of Margaret's glass before she had hold of it. Tiny bits of wine glass scattered over the kitchen floor. Orange juice splattered Margaret's jumper and notepad, and I yelped.

Mums dashed into the kitchen. Mum K began wiping juice off Margaret's left boob, Mum S swept up bits of glass, Margaret pulled a couple of

shards out of her sock, and I sat there clutching
Margaret's pad to my chest saying, 'Oops.'

That's when I noticed all she'd
written on her pad today was this:

B.U.G.
MEETING 2:
CREATIVE
FUNNY
IMAGINATIVE
HONEST?
WELL MANNERED

I DID NOT like that question
mark one bit.
'I made it myself,' I whispered.

'What?' asked Mum.

'My certificate. I've never won Star of the Week
in Class Five. I made the certificate myself.'

Margaret glanced at Mums. Mums squinted at
me. I looked at the floor and then pelted upstairs.

A few minutes later, I heard Margaret leave.
Mum K came upstairs with my fake certificate.
She'd signed it. 'You know you're our star **every**
week, don't you?' she said.

I cried and told her how sorry I was for completely ruining our chances of adopting my baby sister by forgetting to draw her in our first meeting, and then telling a white lie and soaking Margaret's boob in our second.

Mum shook her head and told me not to be silly. She said Margaret had been impressed I'd owned up about the certificate, and reassured me I'd done nothing that'd prevent us from adopting my sister.

I really, really, really, really, really, really, really hope she's right and that my sister arrives soon; people in my class are going to start thinking I've been making her up.

PS I challenge you to try saying 'really, really' twenty-seven times without it turning into 'willy, willy'!

REALLY, REALLY, REALLY, REALLY, REALLY, WILLY, WILLY . . .

PANTS . . .

Auditions are PANTS and I fear our play is going to be even pantser. Look at this cast list Mr Castle left pinned to the noticeboard today . . .

CHIFFCHAFF'S NEW GAFF
Main Parts

Chiffchaff:	Perry Larkin
Eggless:	Layla Dixon
Daredevil Dove:	Janey McVey
Ozzy the Ostrich:	Elliot Quinn
Robin Redbreast:	Dale Redman
Duddly Muck:	Peace Larkin
Fin the Puffin:	Farida Banerjee
Poorly Pigeon:	Patrick North
Confident Crow:	Coral Munro
Turkey/Narrator:	Billie Upton Green

Everyone else will have lots to do as part of the Nightingales' Chorus or the Owls' Parliament.

Please learn your lines before our next rehearsal!
DC

I don't even know why we had auditions. Apart from Layla (who I'm obviously pleased for) not a single person got the part they wanted. I'm not surprised Mr Castle was nowhere to be seen. He has a lot to answer for.

Elliot was devastated he didn't get the part of the puffin. He'd been looking forward to, in his words, 'channelling my inner seahorse'. The puffin lays an egg during the play, you see, and, according to my brainbox friend, seahorses are the only males in the animal kingdom who actually give birth.

Farida was miserable. She'd been desperate to play the robin so she could show off how well she could whistle.

Dale was grumpy too. I cheered him up by pointing out that the robin gets to breakdance in one of the scenes.

BUT CHIFFCHAFFS ARE BROWN . . .

Despite landing the main part, even Perry was disappointed. He'd really wanted to get the part of the ostrich so he could wear pink tights and lipstick.

Janey McVey's reaction surprised me. I thought she'd be gutted about not getting the leading role. 'Oh, excellent, the dove!' she cooed, flicking one of her bunches. 'I wonder if I'll be able to include a graceful mid-air splits routine in my dance.' Grrr.

I mean, I understand **SOME** of Mr Castle's choices:

Patrick will make a decent Poorly
Pigeon. His nose is constantly snotty,
and he's always hopping, so he'll be
OK pretending he's got a gammy leg.

And Coral will be excellent as Confident Crow. As
we found out last week when a patronizing man
came in to show us how to play dodgeball, she
isn't shy about standing up for herself when it
matters. He crouched beside her, you see, and,
in a voice more suitable for nursery children,
said, 'Would you like to sit at the side and watch

your friends?' Well, quite
rightly, Coral gave him a piece
of her mind. She's one of the
sportiest people in Class Five. In
fact, the only person who can
throw more accurately than her

is Dale. He can get a ball of paper into
a bin from seven metres away
(when Mrs Patterson isn't
looking). Also, Coral's wheelchair
is electric. She can zip about on it like
you wouldn't believe. I'm desperate to
have a go, but ever since Dale zipped it
over Daisy Muirhead's foot last year when Coral
let him sit on her knee, we've all been BANNED
from even touching it.

And Peace will be great as Duddly Muck. Not
just because of her unusually large feet and
fondness for orange trainers. She'll be excellent

at pretending she can't hear Perry when Chiffchaff asks the duck if it'll share its nest. Peace ignores Perry all the time. When I get a sister, I will NEVER ignore her.

But Turkey? HMPH. I'm officially offended. I don't get to sing a single line as a soloist and I'm only in two of the dances. I think I might quit.

SNEAKY MCVEY

Guess what I found out today!

Janey McVey **DID** audition for the part of Daredevil Dove.

According to Layla, when Mr Castle mentioned how important it was that the dove could move gracefully (during the last-chance-saloon workshop Mrs Patterson rudely forced me to miss) Janey immediately ditched her Chiffchaff words and picked up the dove's audition piece instead. **That's** why she'd timetabled herself to go last — to give herself time to create a dance and memorize a new set of lines. Can you believe how sneaky she is?!

Apparently she's going round telling people how handy it is she's a splits expert and how 'utterly terrible' it would've been if ANYONE ELSE had got the part because she feels like she was 'born to play it'.

If today's rehearsal is anything to go by, this is a load of rubbish. She's not even learned half her lines yet. She was so embarrassed when I had to keep reminding her what she was supposed to be saying, she pretended all her (massive) pauses were 'completely on purpose' and that I was 'totally interrupting her acting'.

Anyway, the good news is, Mr Castle was SO impressed I already know the whole script back to front that he took me to one side during the break, gave me half his Wagon Wheel, and requested I take on the role of **CAST**

UNDERSTUDY. Which means if anyone's sick (or dead) when it comes to show week (which, as Mr Castle reminded us tonight, is **ONLY THREE WEEKS AWAY**), I'll be playing their part.

I'M ON IT, MR CASTLE!

I cheered up a bit after that. I cheered up even more when Mr Castle set our final positions for 'Welcome to Beaksville'!

HEART ATTACK?

At the special home this afternoon, Mums were chatting to Great-Nan about Kathleen again when Great-Nan said she wondered whether her long-lost sister likes singing. So, when she wobbled off to the commode, I floated the idea that, instead of spending next weekend sitting in the special-home max-volume TV room, we take Great-Nan to Something-by-the-Sea to find out. Well, I've not heard a peep from that Toby since I invited him and his great-grandma up to ours. Plus, I've been doing a spot of research, and the Something-by-the-Sea beach looks breathtaking on Google Earth.

'Absolutely no way!' snapped Mum K, before describing how turning up on the doorstep of a seventy-year-old woman without warning might give her a heart attack.

GULP. Great-Nan's nearly eighty-three . . .

As suspected, Mum S wasn't COMPLETELY against the idea. She's always up for a trip to the seaside, even when it's blowing a full-on gale. 'It's a lovely idea, Billie,' she said, stroking my hair. 'But it's just not feasible at the moment with everything that's going on. Besides, Margaret Mulvaney's coming to do her "home and pet assessment" next weekend.'

I've no idea what a 'home and pet assessment' is, but if Margaret Mulvaney thinks Mr Paws will be up for a chat after our Sunday-morning countryside stroll, she's going to be bitterly disappointed.

Barmy Raymond was on my side. He thinks Great-Nan and Kathleen getting together is a splendid idea. I almost told him about my surprise-meeting plan until he started talking gibberish about his great-nephew, Cyril, AGAIN. According to Raymond, this Cyril has to walk around with bodyguards because he's so famous. I've checked Google and I can confirm that there are no famous Cyrils in the world anywhere.

PINK WAFERS

EEK! Guess who arrived at our house this afternoon!

The Seasiders! FOUR OF THEM! Kathleen, her daughter Valerie, her grandson Robert and her great-grandson Toby — the one who wrote to me.

Mums couldn't believe it. Thankfully, their politeness took over after a few seconds of being in SHOCK and they invited them

in for a coffee and some leftover aubergine muffins (i.e. all of them).

Kathleen looks a bit like Great-Nan. Her hair's darker and her body's less stooped over, but she

has the same smile and a similar
dress sense. (She didn't make any
jokes about poo or wee.)

Valerie is about
the same age as Granny P,
but she's far more
glamorous and smells
much zestier.

Robert is as tall as a tree, softly spoken, and
has the exact same watch as Mum K.

They're all dead interesting, but my FAVOURITE
long-lost relative is Toby. He's twelve years old

and his 'nice to meet you' present was a family-sized pack of biscuits that included Party Rings and pink wafers.

After a few minutes of watching the adults try to digest Mum's vegetable muffins while they made small talk about how different adoption was 'back in the old days', I took Toby (and the biscuits) into the back garden to play on the trampoline. We got on FABULOUSLY.

When I told Toby his name sounded a bit like TOBLA (**T**he **O**fficial **B**iscuit **L**aw **A**ssociation — of which I am the joint-chief) he even came up with a new law that I will certainly be putting forward at our next meeting.

BISCUIT LAW 12

It is compulsory to divide pink wafers into three distinct layers before any eating commences.

Also, I found out Toby loves Zakk-O almost as much as me! His jaw dropped when I described the day I met Zakk-O face to face and discovered tons of amazing facts about him — including how his favourite biscuits are, in fact, pink wafers. (100% true, BTW. Read my second diary if you don't believe me.)

By the time we ventured back inside, Granny Pauline had arrived. The adults decided she and Mum K should bob to the special home on their own to gently prewarn Great-Nan about the Seasiders being  in town. I didn't whine as this course of action minimized the risk of Great-Nan suffering a heart attack. Toby was thrilled because it meant he and his family could stay in a hotel overnight, so he'll get a day off school tomorrow.

Unfortunately, Mum S refused to book me an adjoining room. Pity. I'd like to have spent more time with my long-lost kind-of cousin (and avoided the lengthy lecture on how I should've left Great-Nan to invite her sister up in her own time).

WHAT WERE YOU THINKING?

Thankfully, when Mum K came home, she reported that Great-Nan isn't cross with me (PHEW) and that she's requested we accompany the Seasiders to the special home after school tomorrow (YAY)!

AWKWARD

I couldn't concentrate on a thing at school today.
(Well, apart from when Mrs Patterson tried to
teach us how to say the months in French, at
which point I learned that shouting 'OOOT!'
at the top of your voice and then falling into
a fit of uncontrollable giggles with your #BFF
is a splendid method of remembering how to
say août — the French
word for *August*.)
Other than that,
my mind kept
wandering to
the long-lost-
sister meeting,
and imagining how, when I meet **my** sister,
I'll undoubtedly run to her
and give her a big sloppy
kiss.

Unfortunately, it didn't quite work out like that for Great-Nan and Kathleen. Great-Nan was having one of her grey-faced wobbly days and couldn't get out of bed, so Kathleen had to perch on the bedside commode to have her first-ever chat with her sister (with its lid on; she wasn't using it).

They did hold hands after a while and both got all teary when Kathleen gave Great-Nan a necklace that used to belong to her birth mum. But, on the whole, it was a bit awkward. To be honest, I was glad when Great-Nan let rip with a THUNDEROUS trump. Watching the Seasiders try to stifle their laughter was hilarious.

To escape the whiff, I took Toby for a little tour of the special home.

We found Barmy Raymond in his bedroom singing 'Love of My Life' (another Zakk-O classic) into a mirror while clasping a photo of Great-Nan to his chest. Raymond told us how excited he is about bringing the love of his life to watch *Chiffchaff*. Apparently he and Great-Nan have plans to steal a tablecloth from the special-home dining room to make a banner with my name on it!

Great-Nan had perked up a bit by the time we wandered back to her bedroom. She and Kathleen were talking about how much they both enjoy singing and watching documentaries about angles. Ha! I mean ANGELS. Wow, how boring would a documentary about angles be?!

We took the Seasiders out for tea before they drove home. To fill a couple of awkward silences, I told them all about *Chiffchaff*. They nodded and smiled TONS, so I asked if they'd like me to get

them tickets to watch. We exchanged email addresses and Toby's dad, Robert, PROMISED he'd check his diary.

Blimey. I wish I'd gone for the part of Chiffchaff now. Not only does Perry have the most lines in the play (which would make their journey worthwhile) but I've been thinking and I could totally have drawn on my life experience to play the role realistically. Chiffchaff is literally ADOPTED by Layla the silkie hen at the end. Why do I always think of these things when it's too late?

GOBBLE, GOBBLE

Janey McVey keeps pulling Layla off to run through the one scene the dove and the silkie hen are in together. According to Janey, it's the **'pivotal moment'** of the play. IT'S **SO** NOT. It lasts forty seconds max, and that includes time for Janey to get her nine prompts. The scene between Layla and Perry, where Chiffchaff finally finds an adult bird who's willing to share their nest, is much more important.

Today I pretended I wasn't bothered about being shooed away again and went to see what Coral and Elliot were up to. They were going through the tricky lines in the Ostrich—Crow argument scene.

SORRY, BILLIE, WE HAVE TO GET THIS RIGHT.

In fact, apart from Dale, who'd been banned from playing outside (for whooping when Mr Epping tripped over his shoelace in assembly!), ALL my friends spent every break rehearsing. I don't have anyone to practise my lines with. Apart from telling parts of the story to the audience, my gobble-gobbles are interspersed throughout the play.

I was so bored by afternoon break I even resorted to volunteering to sharpen pencils (so I could keep Dale company). We spent ages looking through the script, particularly at the Chiffchaff and Duddly Muck lines as both Perry and Peace were absent from school today. I mean, I think they've just got colds, but I wanted Mr Castle to know how COMMITTED I am to my UNDERSTUDY role.

Although Mr Castle was impressed, I hope Perry gets better soon because I've realized I'd actually rather understudy Peace's part than play Chiffchaff. Duddly Muck might not be the main character, but Peace has tons of funny lines, most of which involve SPOONERISMS. A spoonerism, BTW, is a phrase like 'Duddly Muck' where the first sounds of words are mixed up — usually by accident. (Peace's character is actually called Muddly Duck.)

My favourite lines are when Duddly Muck tells Robin Redbreast (Dale) he's lucky he's so small because he'll never be eaten for 'Dunday Sinner'. And when she tells Poorly Pigeon (Patrick) he should go and 'shake a tower' because his gammy leg stinks!

PS I dare you to say 'I like spoonerisms' to a male teacher at your school, and then call him a 'smart fella'!

APPARATUS

  At dinner today me and Layla were having a PRIVATE conversation about how AWESOME it will be when we can go out for pram races with our baby sisters, when Janey McVey decided to poke her nose in.

'You might be waiting a while for that, Layla!' Then she laughed, nudging my #BFF in her ribs. I asked her what she meant, and she said, 'Well, it's been AGES since you told us you had a SISTER, Billie. If it's true, where exactly is she?'

She even did air quotes when she said 'SISTER'. Can you believe how RUDE she is?

I wasn't in the mood for going into the whole foster family/assessment thing AGAIN, so I told Painy McVey in no uncertain terms to keep her nose out of my private business. I'm not sure whether what I said was a swear phrase. To be on the safe side, I won't write it in here. Let's just say it began with 'B' and ended with 'ogoff, Janey'.

I felt particularly irritated, despite it being Friday, until Mr Castle took us in the hall for PE and told us we could get the APPARATUS out.

That cheered me up because Mrs Patterson can never be faffed with the apparatus. Not that she'd ever admit it. She always comes up with excuses like,

'You've all been too noisy for that!' Or: 'Mr Ball said the hall floor isn't clean enough today.'

But we all know it's because she
simply can't be bothered.

FOR TODAY'S PE WE WILL JOG
ON THE SPOT WHILE CHANTING
OUR SIX TIMES TABLE.

Anyway, the first half of the lesson was fun.
Mr Castle let us climb on stuff willy-nilly while
Coral used an iPad to try to
take photos and videos of
'bodies in motion'.

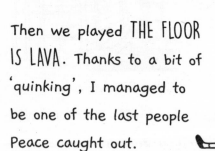

QUICK
THINKING =
QUINKING

Then we played THE FLOOR
IS LAVA. Thanks to a bit of
'quinking', I managed to
be one of the last people
Peace caught out.

But the second half of the lesson went horribly wrong . . .

Mr Castle asked us to get into threes. Just as I was politely declining Perry and Elliot's invitation to accompany them to the upside-down wooden benches to practise balancing (YAWN), Janey McVey GRABBED Layla and Dale, yelled, 'OMG! YES! DREAM TEAM!' then, giving neither of my best friends any choice in the matter, DRAGGED them over to the vault.

After I'd failed to persuade Mr Castle to let me help Coral go around recording 'interesting shapes', the only pair searching for a third member was Patrick and Farida, who'd already claimed the rope. Not only was that a NIGHTMARE TEAM, but I'm rubbish at rope climbing. I mean, I'm not spectacular at vaulting either, but at least that comes with fun accessories — like the mini springboard and the fat crash mat.

Anyway, after a few unsuccessful attempts at shinning up the rope, I left Patrick and Farida arguing about whose pumps were the grippiest, and wandered over to check Dale and Layla weren't missing me too much. Imagine my surprise when I found them laughing their heads off at Painy McVey's STUPID and EXTREMELY SHOWY—OFFY trick of being able to hurdle the vault, sing the dove's solo AND do the splits all at the same time.

DOIN' THE NOSEDIVE JIVE!

It was when she flounced off the crash mat, smirking at me instead of looking where she was going, that my Friday got even worse. Janey tripped over my foot, flung herself on to the floor and clutched her ankle as though she'd fallen off the top of Blackpool Tower. I tried not to laugh, but I couldn't help myself. Janey glared at me, then screamed, 'MR CAAAAAAASTLE! I think I've broken my leg!'

Then, when our teacher sprinted over, she pointed at me and yelled, '**SHE** did it on purpose! She stuck her foot out to trip me because she's the understudy. She knows she'll get to play the dove in *Chiffchaff* if I've got a broken leg!'

Can you believe it?

As I said to Mr Castle in response to his frowny glare, **CROSS MY HEART AND HOPE TO FLY**, it was a **COMPLETE ACCIDENT**. The problem is, I'm not sure he believed me.

Even worse, I'm not sure my friends did either. 'That was so mean of you, Billie,' said Layla, crouching to comfort Janey when Mr Castle dashed off to find an accident form.

'She said "hope to fly",' jeered Patrick North. 'That proves she's dying to be the dove!'

'You didn't even say sorry!' snapped Layla, who 100% knows I've never said 'hope to DIE' since my grandpa told me it was tempting fate.

'BECAUSE I'VE GOT NOTHING TO SAY SORRY FOR!'
I yelled.

Elliot and Dale dragged me into the classroom to calm down after that, but then Mr Castle cancelled Golden Time and everyone glared at me as though it was my fault!

I'm so glad it's Friday. With any luck, the weekend will give Janey enough time to get over her embarrassment and then she and Layla will be the ones apologizing to ME.

DISASTER

We dashed out to HOME—N—GARDEN straight after breakfast this morning. As far as shopping on a Sunday morning goes, HOME—N—GARDEN is not usually the worst place to be dragged out to.

Today, however, wasn't usual.

FOR ONE, Mums were in frantic moods. Our traditional HOME—N—GARDEN game of hide-and-seek was off the agenda, and they wouldn't even let me get into any of the baths. In fact, all they wanted to do was quickly locate a range of odd items they thought Margaret Mulvaney might check for during her afternoon 'home and pet assessment'.

FOR TWO, I ended up being snapped at by a woman with short silver hair who, I swear, must have raided Grandpa's wardrobe this morning — from behind they could've been twins. Oops.

HI, GRANDPA! FOUND ANYTHING EXCITING?

(In my defence, HOME—N—GARDEN is one of Grandpa's favourite places to while away his weekends, and What's in the Fridge? is one of our joint favourite HOME—N—GARDEN activities.)

And, **FOR THREE**, the whole trip made me worry my new baby sister has a reputation for being a fire starter or a thief.

STUFF WE BOUGHT

A MINI FIRE EXTINGUISHER

A SAFE

SOME PADLOCKS

A NEW FIRST-AID KIT

Anyway, Margaret Mulvaney turned up at our door only half an hour after we'd returned. As Mums were still busy installing safety contraptions in the kitchen, they asked me to entertain her for a few minutes. Which I did — by answering all the pet-assessment questions without telling a single white lie. Margaret seemed satisfied Mr Paws will be no danger to my sister when I explained he never bites, he only barks if we play the melodica, and he's pooed indoors just once in his life (behind the TV when a firework scared him).

Mums took over when Margaret said she needed to conduct a quick safety check of our house. Thankfully, we passed the 'home and pet assessment' with flying colours. In fact, I think we might get a certificate as Margaret said we

were the first family she'd ever come across
with a fire blanket in their downstairs loo and
their fruit locked in a safe.

Although this means we're another step closer
to becoming a family of four (YAY), I'm not
particularly pleased with our 'baby-proofed'
house.

FOR ONE, all the keys are now
hanging on hooks just out of my
reach — I have to ask every time
I want to go into the back garden.

FOR TWO, despite me trying to train him for an
hour after tea, Mr Paws is still unable to open

the baby gate at the
bottom of the stairs,
so I've lost my STAY-
AWAKE DOODLE DIARY
bedtime buddy.

And **FOR THREE** (most disastrous of all), the
treat cupboard (which I used to be able to access
by standing on a chair) is now near impossible to
open without making a ton of
noise or dislocating two
fingers as EVERY kitchen
cabinet has been fitted with
a stupid safety catch.

Oh well, at least my knicker
drawer wasn't baby-proofed;

my emergency jelly
babies remain safe.

PS Margaret didn't
mention my fake
certificate. She didn't even ask about the real
one I'd magnetted to the fridge. Probably just
as well, TBH. I got it
for 'splendid sitting'
when I was in Class One.

AWARDED TO
BILLIE
FOR SPLENDID SITTING

99%

When I saw Janey McVey
hobbling into the line this
morning, I realized I'd been
wrong to think Friday's PE
incident would be forgotten.

She's such an overdramatic
attention-seeker. Her ankle isn't even swollen.
Plus, I'm sure I saw her put her full weight on
her foot in assembly when she thought no one
was looking.

Even Mrs Patterson gave her TONS of sympathy.
She allowed her to sit with her leg up during
lessons, AND let her choose who she wanted to
sit beside in case she needed help going to the
toilet! I wasn't at all surprised when Janey
picked Layla, but I couldn't stop worrying she
might spend the day continuing to try to convince

my #BFF I'd tripped her on purpose. **Which I didn't.**

I was right. Every time Mrs Patterson turned her back, Janey started whispering into my #BFF's ear. I tried to ignore Painy's sly glances, but when Layla didn't reply to ANY of the notes I slipped her during maths, I realized I had a MAJOR problem.

WHAT HAVE YOU GOT FOR SNACK?

Sorry you've been lumbered with Painy. What is she whispering about?

She'd better not still be saying I tripped her up on purpose.

WHAT'S THE ANSWER TO NUMBER THREE?

R U OK?

Y R U IGNORING ME?

By break I was desperate to ask Layla what
Janey had been saying about me (and swap half
my carrot sticks for whatever tasty delight
Layla's mum had packed her) but
the pair of them didn't even
come outside.

In fact, the first chance I got
to speak to my so-called #BFF
without Painy McVey stuck to her side was
in the cloakroom at home time.

'Had a rubbish day?' I asked, hoping Layla would
apologize for what she'd said on Friday and tell
me how terrible being Janey's water-bottle-
fetcher and door-opener had been.

I was not expecting her reply. 'Stop being mean,
Billie,' she snapped. 'Just admit you tripped
Janey on purpose so she might not be able to
play the dove, and tell her you're sorry.'

I **KNEW** Janey was still trying to get Layla to believe her lies. 'But I didn't!' I semi-shouted. 'It was an accident. What am I supposed to apologize for, having feet?'

'Stop trying to be funny,' growled Layla. 'If you don't apologize soon, Janey's going to tell Mrs Patterson, and then you'll be in BIG trouble.'

I worried about that until teatime. My main concern being if Janey's completely convinced Layla — my best friend in the whole world who's known me FOREVER — that I tripped her on purpose, she'll easily be able to use her slimy teacher's-pet-ness to convince Mrs Patterson, who'll no doubt force Mr Castle to sack me, and I'll end up not being in the play at all.

At teatime I realized I had a lot more to lose than a part in a play.

'You might see Margaret Mulvaney in school tomorrow lunchtime,' announced Mum S.

I asked why. Mum said it was nothing to worry about but that, as part of our adoption ASSESSMENT, our social worker has to chat with my teacher about how I'm getting on at school. At that point my heart began beating like an abscess and I burst into tears. 'She'll tell Margaret not to let us adopt my sister,' I cried.

'What? Why?' asked Mum, her forehead wrinkling.

I told Mum the whole story — about PE and Janey falling over, and what Layla's been like and how Janey's planning to get me into trouble by telling Mrs Patterson I tripped her on purpose because I'm desperate to understudy the dove. 'Did you do it on purpose?' asked Mum, lowering her chin and raising her eyebrows.

That made me have a little think. On Friday I was 100% sure I didn't. But, after the way Layla's been acting, I'm more like 99% now. What if I did and I can't remember? I **was** in a bit of a bad mood. And I **would** rather be playing the dove than the turkey.

'Billie . . .?' said Mum.

'I don't know any more,'
I admitted. 'Layla thinks
I did.'

Mum put her arm round me. She
said if there's any possibility, however small, that
what Janey is saying might be true, I should
probably apologize — just to be on the safe side.
She also reminded me that Margaret Mulvaney
would be more impressed with someone who can
admit their mistakes than someone who tries to
cover them up.

I'm not exactly thrilled about the prospect of
apologizing for something I'm only 1% sure I did,
but for the sake of my nearly-here baby sister,
I'm probably going to do it.

URGH.

100%

My heart sank when I walked into class this morning, only to find Janey already at Mrs Patterson's desk. I couldn't hear what they were talking about, but, as Janey kept squeezing out fake tears and clutching her ankle, I assumed she was telling her lies.

After a few minutes, Mrs Patterson called me to her desk to join them. Everyone else went deadly silent. I could practically feel fifty-six eyes

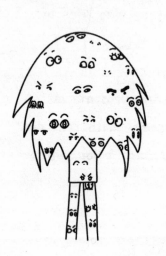 boring into my back. Crossing my fingers that a confession would work in my favour when Mrs Patterson had her chat with Margaret Mulvaney later in the day, I took a deep breath and said, at the speed of one of those

announcers who say a billion words at the end of radio adverts, 'There's-a-one-per-cent-chance-I-might've-tripped-Janey-on-purpose-in-PE-on-Friday.'

A few tuts came from around the class. Mrs Patterson looked confused. Janey stared at the floor. 'I'm sorry about your ankle, Janey,' I added. 'I hope it's better before the opening night of *Chiffchaff* because —'

At that point Mrs Patterson held up her hand.

'Billie,' she said, 'as I've been telling Janey here, Mr Castle emailed me last night. He's eager for me to share with the pair of you a video Coral captured during your PE lesson on Friday.'

Me and Janey both swung our heads round to look

over at Coral. Along with the rest of the class, she sat in silence, pretending to read.

In the meantime, Mrs Patterson had opened an iPad at a file labelled 'PE: Movement Videos'. Her finger hovered over a thumbnail that looked like Janey midway through her vaulty-singing-splitsy ~~manoover~~ ~~manoovre~~ performance.

'She didn't trip me,' mumbled Janey. 'I fell over her foot by accident.'

EVERYONE gasped. Mrs Patterson shut the iPad. (Disappointing — I'd like to have seen Janey McVey floor-plant again.)

'I'm sorry for what I said,' whispered Janey, her face tomato-red.

I turned to look at Layla. She looked mortified. That's when I decided the best thing to do was to put the whole thing behind us (and give Mrs Patterson something amazing to tell Margaret when she saw her later in the day). 'It's OK, Janey,' I said, offering her my hand to shake. Mrs Patterson BEAMED at me. RESULT! Then she turned to Janey. 'I think it might do you good to sit outside the office at break time instead of staying inside with Layla,' she said. 'Now go and sit down.'

My #BFF was full of apologies at playtime. 'I'm so sorry, Billie,' she said, sobbing. 'I should've known you wouldn't lie to me.'

I forgave her in an instant. Well, the instant

after she gave me the
whole of her Cheestring in
exchange for a hard pear.

PS I'm now 99% sure Janey's
been making her ankle appear
TONS worse than it is. At tonight's
rehearsal, not only did she keep forgetting to
limp, she performed an actual cartwheel during
Farida's rendition of 'Find Me a Fish'. In all
honesty I feel sorry for her. If you have to
pretend your ankle is sore to get attention, and
tell lies to get someone to be your friend, you
must be desperate.

GREASY HAIR

Margaret Mulvaney's been again.

It was our final meeting and she was in an extra-speedy mood. I'd barely sat down when she said, 'What three words would you use to describe yourself, Billie?'

I like rapid-fire games. I'm the quickest at **X or Y?** in my class. You know the game where someone gives you two options and you have to say your preference without thinking. No? OK, let's play it now. From each pair, you have one second to choose your favourite:

 BATH OR SHOWER?

 DOGS OR CATS?

 ART OR PE?

 PIZZA OR CHIPS?

 TV OR READING?

 SICK OR POO?

 JAFFA CAKE OR CHOCOLATE DIGESTIVE?

 METAL OR PLASTIC?

 SWING OR SLIDE?

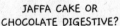 CLEVER OR CUTE?

 LAYLA OR DALE?

 ZAKK-O OR MR EPPING?

Some are easier than others, as you'll have noticed.

Anyway . . . I said KIND, HONEST and FUNNY. Then, to prove these things, I:

1. **KINDLY** offered her a biscuit. Unfortunately, she declined so I didn't get a chance to show her how ridiculous having a baby lock on an already out-of-reach cupboard is. (Unless my new sister can fly . . .)

2. Mentioned (very **HONESTLY**) that I thought her hair needed washing. (She frowned.)

3. Told her a semi-**FUNNY** (but appropriately speedy) cake joke. (She fake-smiled.)

WHAT'S THE FASTEST CAKE IN THE WORLD?

S'GONE!

Next, she asked me if I had any bad points.
So I admitted I'm sometimes a bit too honest
and that my jokes are not always funny. This
made Margaret laugh! It also prompted her to
tell me that Mrs Patterson had said much the
same thing during their little chat! According to
Margaret, Mrs P also mentioned how marvellous I
am at helping younger children when they fall in
the playground. Although this is 100% true, it
mostly involves me helping infants hobble to the
bench or going inside for wet paper towels. Still,
I didn't correct Margaret when she overpraised

me as though I regularly
administer life-saving
injections. (I must
remember to be extra
nice to Mrs P this week.)

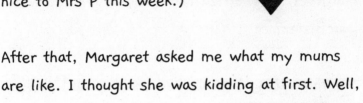

After that, Margaret asked me what my mums
are like. I thought she was kidding at first. Well,
for one, she's met them many times. And, for

two, if she needed extra information, she could've just shouted to them — they were both in the living room. Maybe it was her sneaky way of seeing if I'd reveal they have a history of dropping babies or something? (They don't . . . I don't think.) Anyway, I told her all sorts of interesting stuff I thought Mums might have forgotten to mention.

MUM S LIKES SAVING MONEY AND SHE'S FRIGHTENED OF FROGS.

MUM K CAN JUGGLE AND SHE'S SCARED OF BUBBLE WRAP.

'Are **YOU** scared about anything, Billie?' asked Margaret. 'Or worried about anything to do with your sister?'

The main thing I'm worried about is us FAILING our ASSESSMENT and my sister having to go and

live with strangers. I kept that to myself,
though. I didn't want to be asked for a quick
rundown of reasons why my sister **shouldn't**
come and live with me. Shaking my head, I
stared at my hands for a minute, waiting for
my next question.

'I've only got one mum, Billie,' said Margaret.
'What's it like having two?'

'Margaret,' I said, 'all families are
different, but love is the same.'

'That's a very grown-up response, Billie,' said
Margaret. 'But, tell me the truth, have you
ever been bullied or picked on for having
two mums?'

I shook my head before telling Margaret I've not
been bullied, but that sometimes people make
odd comments, or ask me tons of nosy questions,

or tell me 'You can't have two mums' (like Janey once said).

'And what do you say to them?' she asked.

So I told her I always answer them honestly, and try to make them understand that: yes, you **CAN** have two mums; it's entirely normal; and I am, in fact, living proof.

Margaret wrote a lot of notes about this in her book. She said I'd be an EXCELLENT AVOCADO for my new sister. She smiled too, so I took that to be a compliment.

Margaret's non-stop questions were exhausting me. When she asked for my thoughts on sharing, I told her briefly about how I regularly share my snack with Layla (without mentioning how my #BFF's goodies are always tons better

than mine) and my game ideas with Dale
(without saying this usually occurs during
morning lessons).

'Can you think of anything you might be able to
share if your sister comes to live with your
family?' asked Margaret.

I hated the way she said 'if'. She's MY sister.
There should be no ifs or maybes about
it. Anyway, I said my reading book
and my vegetables, as I know babies
like stories and mushy food. Margaret laughed as
though I'd made a joke, so I thought for a long
time and said I'd also share my knowledge of
how to deal with narrow-minded people with my
new sister when she gets a bit older.

'What do you mean by that?' asked Margaret.
So I told her how sometimes people call Perry
Larkin names simply because he's a boy who

likes playing with dolls and wearing pink. But I always stand up for him and remind all the meanies how everyone is different, and that I'll teach my sister never to judge anybody on anything other than the way they treat you.

'I liked the way you shared your biscuits with me at our first meeting,' I added, hoping Margaret would suddenly remember she'd brought a packet of something delicious I could teach her how to eat properly.

She didn't. She said, 'I'm trying to lose a bit of weight at the moment. But I have an apple if you're hungry.'

Hang on a sec . . .

SILENT LETTERS

Sorry about that. Mum K just room-invaded to
ask me why I'd written custard creams on the
shopping list twelve times. Despite it being
almost 9 p.m., she smiled when she saw me
practising spellings, so my QUINKING worked.

After she'd given me a silent-p word (which I suspect she invented to make herself look cleverer), she asked me if I felt any calmer.

You see, before Margaret went home, she said, 'I'll be taking your mums to see PANEL on Friday.'

'Who's Panel?' I asked, wondering if that might be my new baby sister's name. That's when I found out some UTTERLY FRUSTRATING information, which made me throw a cushion at the door (when Margaret had gone).

This is the thing: although we've finished all our ASSESSMENT chats, and I think I've done a reasonable job convincing Margaret I'm going to be a super-duper avocado, she's not even the person who gets to say YES or NO to my sister coming to live with us.

ARGH!

In actual fact, a group of adoption experts (called PANEL) have to check all Margaret's meeting notes. Then on Friday Mums have to go to a mega-important meeting so this PANEL can ask them even more questions and check Margaret hasn't forgotten anything. And it's this PANEL that decides whether or not my new sister is finally allowed to move from her Bourbon Heaven House and join our family forever.

As I told Mum, I **am** feeling calmer now, but earlier I had a mega worry that someone on this PANEL might say no if Margaret's notes mention my fake certificate (or her juicy boob), especially since I've not been invited to defend myself.

I sincerely hope these PANEL people say yes (and don't test Mum K on silent-p words). Not just because I already love my sister (weird considering I've never even met her) but I also want to plonk her on Janey McVey's disbelieving head (preferably when she's done a pooey nappy).

PS I'm glad PANEL said yes when I was a baby or who knows where I'd be? I can't imagine not being with my mums . . .

PPS I've just checked something with Mum. I'm going to be a 'super ADVOCATE' for my sister, not an avocado. An advocate, FYI, is someone who will always support you — which I will (unless she asks me to start eating avocado).

INITIATIVE

Mrs Patterson partnered me with Janey for English this morning. I think she could tell Janey needed a friend. Everyone's been a bit off with her since the whole false accusation / fake injury episode.

As I wasn't in the mood for investigating 'words with double letters', and all Janey could think of was 'reaLLy', 'soRRy' and 'BiLLie', I broke the tension between us by sharing my exciting news.

MY SISTER MIGHT BE ARRIVING TOMORROW.

After I'd explained about Mums' important PANEL meeting, Janey apologized for insinuating my sister didn't exist. She said her recent moodiness has been Patrick's fault. Apparently every time she asks him to run through their scene, he just makes fart noises with his armpits and it's stressing her out. Patrick is annoying, but I'm pretty sure he isn't to blame for any of Janey's meanness or lies. However, as she suggested we ask Mr Castle if a few turkey lines could be inserted into the dove—pigeon scene so I could help her deal with Patrick, I decided not to contradict her.

I was completely on board, you see, with ramping up my acting time. I mean, I'm on stage LOADS, but that's mostly to tell the audience things or hold up signs. So I said I'd have a little think. Which I did

A FEW DAYS LATER . . .

during history — at which
point I had a brainwave.

At playtime I gathered the whole cast, told them
my idea and, by the end of the day, we'd
devised a whole new impressive scene to replace
the dove–pigeon one, which we'll be showing
Mr Castle at tomorrow's rehearsal.

It starts with Elliot (Ozzy the
Ostrich) offering everyone a jelly
snake before leaving the packet
with me (as the narrator).

Then Peace (Duddly Muck) comments on the
unseasonable 'rack of lain'. This leads to me
(as the turkey) and Dale
(Robin Redbreast)
performing an intricate
rain dance.

After that, I ask Farida (the puffin who's about
to lay another egg) if she's
thought about baby
names. She says she's
going to call her sixth
puffling 'FAB' (obvs).

Patrick (gammy-legged pigeon) then squawks
to Farida that her ankles look swollen and
offers to lend her his spare walking stick.

I MIGHT BE A WHILE.
I LEFT IT IN TRAFALGAR
SQUARE . . .

Next, Coral (Confident Crow) caws to Layla
(Eggless the silkie hen) that she should look on
the bright side of egglessness, and think herself

lucky she'll never have the bodily issues of
pregnancy to deal with.

Finally, I explain to Perry (Chiffchaff) that,
although I don't have room in my
turkey nest for him, I do have
space for an iPad. So Janey
(Daredevil Dove) nosedives
away to fetch me hers
(which I play on while the
next scene goes on).

The way I see it, we've still got two weeks before
showtime. Everyone pretty much knows their lines,
we're all perfect at the songs, and the dances are
almost flawless, so we could do with something
new to stop rehearsals being too repetitive.

I don't know what Mr Castle will say, but I
expect he'll be DELIGHTED as he's usually
impressed when people use their **INITIATIVE**.

MORE WAITING . . .

Mums took me to Granny Pauline's before school because they had to drive a long way to get to PANEL. Granny P was all teary, saying she

 couldn't wait to meet my new sister and how she wishes her mum (Great-Nan) had known about **her** sister sooner.

All day while we made masks for the Nightingales' Chorus and Owls' Parliament my mind kept wandering.

First I worried about Mrs Satnav and whether

TURN ROUND WHEN POSSIBLE!

PANEL PLACE

she might make Mums late if she was in one of her narky moods. Then I panicked

Margaret might warn the PANEL people I'm dropsy with wine glasses, but forget to mention how life-saving Mrs P told her I am with little ones.

CLEAR THE AREA!
I COME EQUIPPED WITH
A WET PAPER TOWEL.

Finally I feared PANEL would hate the picture of my baby sister as ~~a smudge of yellow felt-tip~~ a shining star in our hearts so much that they might say NO.

Anyway, as soon as Drama Club finished this evening I ran out to the yard. Both mums were waiting for me. 'How did it go?' I asked.

'Well,' said Mum K.

'Well, what?' I asked, my insides flipping a somersault.

'No! WELL!' said Mum S. 'REALLY well! The panel said YES!'

I clapped my hands and jumped up and down like a hyperactive frog before realizing something VITAL was missing. 'Where is she?' I asked, glancing around to see if they'd put my new sister under the netball posts or anything.

'Still with the Bourbons,' they said.

OMG. You'll never guess what. PANEL saying yes isn't even the last stage of the adoption!
I KNOW!

Next, the PANEL people have to convince **THEIR** boss, the super-duper expert called THE DECISION MAKER, to also say yes. Mums said it's 'just a formality' and we should find out for certain soon, but that we shouldn't 'count our chickens' (which would be impossible considering we don't own any).

I mean, I'm delighted PANEL said yes, but I'm utterly fed up my sister's **STILL** not here. Even though I've never met her, I miss having her in my life. Plus, I told everyone there was a high chance I'd be bringing her in for show-and-tell next week. GRRR.

Oh, I forgot to say — Mr Castle watched the new *Chiffchaff* scene I'd directed. Although he liked our initiative, he said not all the lines were a super fit for the play. As a compromise, he said he'd let me be part of either the Nightingales' Chorus or the Owls' Parliament.

I chose to be an extra owl as:

A. there are only four others
and
B. they get to sing a song with the phrase 'Love is OWL you need' in it.

The show is looking fabulous, BTW. I wish you could come and watch it.

PS I'm not entirely sure what makes this
DECISION MAKER person such a know-it-all,
but I'm certainly going to research this job
for when I'm older.

TOBSTER999

I got an exciting email from Toby today.

To: CustardUnderscoreCream
From: Tobster999
Subject: Urgent!! READ IMMEDIATELY!

Message:

Billie,
I've found out something you won't believe about Zakk-O! I'll tell you when we next come up because I need to see your face when you hear this!

Won't be long, BTW, because, GUESS WHAT, Dad says we can come up and visit Great-Gran's new sister at the same time your bird show is on!!!!!!!!!!!! (Gobble, gobble – can't wait to laugh at you in your turkey costume!)

Dad says he'll text your mums later to let them know my great-gran wants to bring your great-nan and Raymond with us – so we'll need six tickets (for the Thursday night).

See you soon!
Toby ☺

PS Are you mad? Why is the word 'underscore' in your email address? LOLS.

After Robert had texted Mums, I called Great-Nan to tell her the news. It made her day. Her exact words were: 'Good. We'll need to get out of this room next time the Seasiders come. That Kathleen had terrible wind!'

PS There's NO WAY Toby will be able to tell me anything about Zakk-O that I don't already know. I've read EVERY WORD on the official Zakk-O website (and most of the fan-zone ones).

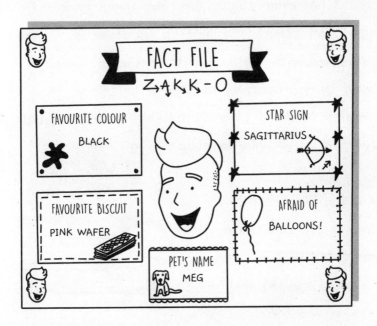

FACT FILE
ZAKK-O

FAVOURITE COLOUR
BLACK

STAR SIGN
SAGITTARIUS

FAVOURITE BISCUIT
PINK WAFER

AFRAID OF
BALLOONS!

PET'S NAME
MEG

KNICKER WINGS

Our weekend homework has been to create our own *Chiffchaff* costumes without spending any money.

As Grandma Jude was busy (and Mums' idea of an amazing turkey costume was to wrap me in a threadbare black towel and put a rubber glove on my head), I decided I'd go over to Layla's to see if her mum could help. Mrs Dixon is an upcycling expert. My #BFF's wardrobe is crammed with quirky outfits (not all of which used to be maternity dresses or curtains). Plus, I wanted to spend time with Neela in case I could learn a bit of baby language.

I did, BTW. 'Prumplur' means 'Hi, Billie. I'm delighted you've come round' (I think) and

PRUMPLUR.

'Brrrrrrda' means 'Oh, you're here too, are you?' (I assume — that's what came out of Neela's mouth when Janey McVey turned up with an intricate design of her ideal dove costume.)

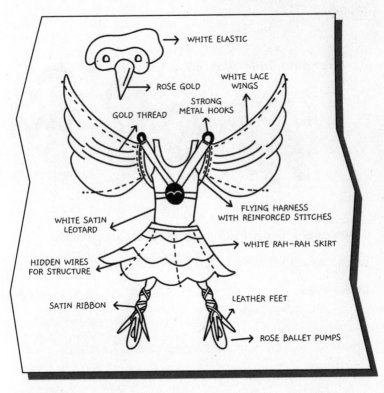

WHITE ELASTIC

WHITE LACE WINGS

ROSE GOLD

STRONG METAL HOOKS

GOLD THREAD

FLYING HARNESS WITH REINFORCED STITCHES

WHITE SATIN LEOTARD

WHITE RAH-RAH SKIRT

HIDDEN WIRES FOR STRUCTURE

LEATHER FEET

SATIN RIBBON

ROSE BALLET PUMPS

While Mrs Dixon set about scrambling materials together, she offered to give us 50p each if we kept Layla's three little brothers out of mischief.

Babysitting is PIPS. All it took was one splendiferous idea from me, and we didn't hear a peep from them for a whole hour.

LAST ONE TO STOP JOGGING ON THE SPOT GETS A BISCUIT!

I sincerely hope Mums employ me regularly when my sister arrives. I could be a MILLIONAIRE in no time.

Anyway, when our costumes were finished, we tried them on one by one.

Janey went first. Mrs Dixon had made her dove outfit from an off-white silk blouse. She'd constructed wings from wire hangers covered in strips of white material (that looked remarkably like cut-up cotton knickers!).

Janey wrinkled her nose.
She said she doubted its armpits would stand the strain when she's heaved off the ground to do her flying splits, and that she'd ask her mum to buy her a 'proper' costume online. Rude. (And against the rules.)

Layla went second. Her silkie-hen outfit is made from three of Neela's fluffy white blankets sewn together and a headband with a toilet-brush topper. It's not perfect, but Layla gave her mum a huge hug and said thank you. Because, unlike Janey, she's not an ungrateful madam.

I went last and (phew) my turkey costume is 100% the best of the three. Take a look at this beauty. I gave Mrs Dixon her 50p back as payment for her effort and told her I loved it.

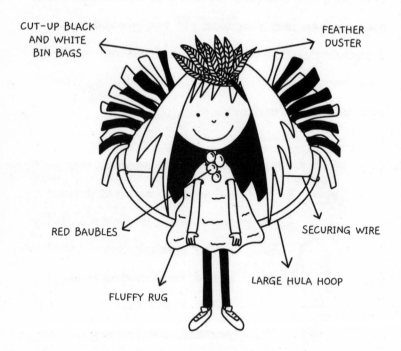

CUT-UP BLACK
AND WHITE
BIN BAGS

FEATHER
DUSTER

RED BAUBLES

SECURING WIRE

LARGE HULA HOOP

FLUFFY RUG

HUN

Mr Castle's #BFF came to watch our *Chiffchaff* rehearsal today. His name is Reef and he's a theatre critic, which basically means he gets FREE TICKETS to watch local shows that he then writes about in newspapers and on websites. (Another job that might suit me when I'm older.) We didn't perform the whole show for Reef, only the musical numbers. He wrote lots of notes. I expect they were all complimentary because I heard him say,

'It's breathtaking, hun,' to Mr Castle (which made 'hun' blush with pride).

My favourite part of tonight's rehearsal, though, was our costume parade. Everyone looked FANTASTIC, but my top three (excluding my own) were:

1. Elliot's ostrich — he had INCREDIBLE mechanical wings, and he looked hilarious in a pair of bright pink tights and his aunty Eileen's big pink fluffy slippers. (Perry is so jealous.)

2. Coral's crow — she had a HUGE black sheet that covered her whole wheelchair, an amazing gold beak and two amusingly large cardboard wings.

3. Patrick's pigeon — it's dead simple but I loved the IRIDESCENT scarf he'd wrapped round his neck and the fake plaster cast his mum had created for his gammy leg.

I CAN'T WAIT for the actual dress rehearsal. Well, not only am I interested to see how we look on the set (which the non-acting members of Class Five have nearly finished painting), but Mr Castle said we're doing it on Friday morning and, if it all goes well, we can spend the WHOLE AFTERNOON playing daft games.

PS Daredevil Dove isn't having a flying harness of any sort and Mr Castle said Janey's knicker-blouse ensemble is PERFECT! HA.

THRANIMAL

We bobbed over to see Great-Nan after
rehearsals tonight. I think she might be
forgetting to take her pills. She called Mum S
'Nicholas', accused Mum K of stealing her
helicopter and tried to eat Page 4 of my
Chiffchaff script. It would've
been funny, but when
she had no idea what
I was talking about
when I mentioned
the Seasiders'
upcoming visit and
forgot to smile when
I told her my own
nearly-here sister is very nearly here, I got a
funny feeling in my tummy and left Mums to it
in favour of going for a wander.

Unfortunately, Barmy Raymond had gone out with a relative, the special-home cook hadn't made any of her super-fantastic Tuesday Treats, and the news was on in the TV room, so it wasn't a great visit overall.

I worried about Great-Nan until we got home and I saw a letter on the doormat addressed to me. Assuming it was from Toby, I opened it carefully in case it contained a couple of ten-pound notes to pay for the Seasiders' six *Chiffchaff* tickets (or more clues about this secret fact he thinks he knows about Zakk-O).

But, guess what, it wasn't from Toby at all . . . It was from . . .

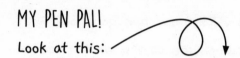

MY PEN PAL!
Look at this:

10 DOWNING STREET
LONDON SW1A 2AA

Dear Billie,

I'm writing to address your request that the English language be overhauled to aid your spelling-test results. It is with sadness that, again, I am unable to help.

With regard to the word 'thranimal', you might be interested to know that if an invented word is used by enough people over a period of time, it has a chance of being added to dictionaries. 'OMG', for example, was added in 2011 after such activity.

I too struggle with spelling, but I have never let it stop me following my dreams. Keep trying and, who knows, one day you could be running our great country.

Best wishes,
The prime minister

PS Your play sounds wonderful, but I'm afraid I don't think I'm going to be able to make it. Break a leg!

OMG. Layla is going to be so excited. THRANIMAL has a chance of becoming an actual word!

And double OMG. 'I **DON'T THINK**' is not '**NO**'.

PS According to Mums, 'break a leg' means 'do so well that people don't just clap at the end, they stomp their legs so hard they cause themselves a mischief'. Weird.

WONDER WEDNESDAY!

Until a couple of hours ago I planned to spend this bedtime writing about how impressed everyone was when I showed them my letter from the prime minister. Well, apart from Janey McVey who said FLYPITS (flying splits) would be a much better word for the world to add to their vocabulary than THRANIMAL (err, nope).

Wondering what could be more exciting than everyone (even Mrs Patterson) disagreeing with Janey McVey? I'll tell you.

Margaret Mulvaney's been on the phone and guess what . . .

THE MAN IN CHARGE OF MAKING THE **FINAL** DECISION ABOUT ADOPTIONS HAS SAID:

YES!

Which means . . .

I'M 100% ABSOLUTELY DEFINITELY GETTING A NEW SISTER!!!!!!!!!!!!!!!!!!! WHOOOOOOOOOOOOOOOOOOOOOOOOOOOOOOP!!!!!!!!!!!!!!!

Her name is Hadbury and **I CANNOT WAIT** to finally meet her!

Unfortunately, I have to . . . Although she's **100%** going to be part of our family, Margaret refused to allow us to go to collect her and bring her home immediately. Apparently we have to do something called 'LINKING', which means us getting to know each other at the Bourbon house. I completely understand why — it'd be a bit of a shock if we just marched in and brought her home before she'd even got to know our names. We're doing this LINKING on Saturday, so on the positive side I only have two days to wait. I just hope it doesn't take **ALL** day. Not *just* because I might miss *Saleema Selective: High-School*

Detective — I also want to bring her home and show her round and dress her in cute clothes and take her to Layla's so we can start as we mean to go on.

PS No, I've never heard the name Hadbury before either, but I like it a lot. It reminds me of a bar of chocolate. Mums said they'll probably shorten it to Haddie — like they always say Billie instead of Belinda. Either way, she's already luckier than me: H.U.G. = 100% awesome initials.

SMELLY STUFF

I can't write much tonight because I've been
instructed to find 'something smelly' we can put
in Haddie's cot on Saturday so she can quickly
get used to my AROMA. (Rude — I shower every
other day.)

Mum K says she's
taking a blanket she's
been sleeping with for
a few weeks (weird).

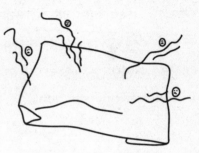

Mum S is taking a T-shirt
she forgot to put in the linen
basket (gross).

They suggested
I take Kyle — he's my koala from
Australia that Aunty Sal bought me
when I was two and who I sleep

with every night. I'm not sure about giving Kyle to Haddie in case she slobbers on him (I've witnessed Neela drooling like a hungry dog on her bib), so I've decided to take my third-favourite cuddly toy: Noodle Von Wooferson. NVW probably smells of me a bit because last week I used him as a cushion at my desk when I wanted to be seated slightly higher. I'm 50% sure I didn't trump on him.

Poor Haddie — she's not going to know what's hit her with all the new pongs going up her nose.

BLINDED . . .

We had our *Chiffchaff* dress rehearsal at school
this morning.

It was TERRIBLE. Everyone (including me) forgot
loads of their lines, Perry
barfed in Coral's nest,
and Dale almost got
blinded by one of
Elliot's mechanical
wings and had to go
home before the
interval.

According to Mr Castle, we're not to worry
because it's a theatre tradition that if a dress
rehearsal goes pear-shaped, the real performance
will be PERFECT. I sincerely hope he's right. I
also hope Dale's eye improves over the weekend.
I mean, I was word-perfect as the understudy

robin for the second half,
but I'm not sure I'll be able to
learn how to whistle by Tuesday.

PFFT!

Despite the hiccups, Mr Castle still let us have
Friday-afternoon Golden Time, most of which we
spent playing a new game called ~~Youneek~~
~~Yewneak~~ Exclusive Pictures. Basically we had to
divide a piece of paper into six squares. When

Mr Castle shouted a letter of the
alphabet, we had twenty seconds
to draw something beginning with
that letter in one of our boxes.

Points were awarded like this:
- **TEN** points if no one had drawn the same
  thing as you.
- **FIVE** points if only one other person had
  drawn the same thing as you.
- **ONE** point if you'd drawn the same as many
  other people.

- And **ZERO** if you'd drawn something completely invalid.

I was the only person to score **SIXTY** points. See if you can beat me. Draw something beginning with the letter in each square . . .

P	G
K	W
T	H

Good effort, but if you drew any foods, common animals, buildings or someone we all know in any of your squares, I can say with certainty you'd only have got one point for it. Here's a winning example:

Pterodactyl	Gnat
Knitting	Wren
Tsunami	Honest

(I guess that silent-letter nonsense came in handy after all!)

The absolute best thing about today, though, was when Margaret Mulvaney popped over after tea to give us directions to the Bourbon house. She'd brought me a congratulations card. Inside it was . . .

A PHOTO OF HADDIE!

Just a sec . . . My early-warning system has been triggered — I ~~strateajicly~~ ~~strateegicly~~ carefully placed seven pieces of Lego on the bottom step of our stairs when I noticed Mums had no shoes on . . .

WARNING!

It worked! Mum yelling 'SUGAR BUTTIES!' gave me plenty of time to turn off my torch, hide my diary and pretend to be asleep.

So, where was I? Oh yes, the photo of MY ACTUAL BABY SISTER! As you'll have noticed, she **looks** uber-cute. However, as I was reminded a few hours ago, appearances can be deceiving . . .

We went out, you see, for an 'OMG, we're finally going to meet Haddie tomorrow' celebration tea. When we arrived at the cafe, Mum S took me to the counter and announced I could order ANYTHING AT ALL.

OMG. I love nearly having a baby sister. Usually I'm only allowed to look at the cakes or ice creams **after** I've finished every last morsel of something Mums consider healthy, and even then they always try to get me to go thirds on a treat with them.

CAN I HAVE A PIECE OF THAT?

WE'LL SEE. YOU MIGHT NOT BE HUNGRY AFTER YOUR BROCCOLI PIE.

So, taking advantage of my last-ever outing as an only child (I know — yikes, right?!) I peered in the glass cabinet and immediately spotted a scrumptious-looking chocolate cake. It had a sign next to it that said **TASTE OF HEAVEN** in large enticing letters.

'I'll have an extra-large slice of that, please, Mr Cafe Man,' I said, drooling at the thought of JUST chocolate cake for tea.

'Wait a minute,' interrupted Mum, pointing at a ton of tiny writing beneath the Taste of Heaven name. 'Read the whole label, Billie. I don't think you'll like that one.'

Three thoughts rushed through my mind at this point:

1. Mum can be SNEAKY. She attempts to cram additional reading into every possible situation. This was obviously one of those moments.

2. Was Mum already REGRETTING her unhealthy 'Haddie is almost here' generosity, and thinking she should've forced me to eat brown bread and mushrooms before allowing me to stuff my face with chocolate heaven?

3. Cake-eating should NEVER involve reading — FACT.

So I secretly rolled my eyes at the GENIUS baker behind the counter, shook my head and said, 'I don't need to read all that, Mum. The cake is called "Taste of Heaven" and just look at it!'

Here's a summary of what happened next:

1. Mum bought it (and GASPED when she realized it cost £3.75).
2. I took a HUGE bite.

3. Mums STARED at me
   with weird expectant
   eyes.
4. I PRETENDED
   I loved the
   vile mush in
   my mouth
   for about two
   and a half seconds.

   MMMM.
5. I SPAT it into a napkin.
6. The man behind the
   counter stared at me with
   a wicked little grin on his
   face as though he was actually
   an EVIL baker whose sole
   purpose in life was to bake
   vomit-inducing overpriced
   confectionery that tastes of
   coffee-flavoured pigsty mud.
7. Mum bought me a cookie and ate the
   remainder of the cake herself. (I suspect

that's why she bought it — she loves coffee-flavoured anything, even jelly.)

Anyway, I guess what I'm trying to say is: you should NEVER judge ANYTHING on appearance alone. Don't say you haven't been warned. I'll tell you what Haddie is like when I've met her in person.

ARGH,
THAT'S
TOMORROW!!!!!!!!!!!!

DEN

Nothing much to report.

JOKES!!!

I met MY SISTER today!

In summary:
She's SUPER cute, MEGA loud, and her current favourite hobbies are: crying, pooing, sleeping and sicking up bits of frothy spit. I love her.

In longgary:
We set off straight after breakfast and arrived at the Bourbon house after driving for almost an hour. (I was so EXCITED — I even lost at Mini Punch for the first time in my life.)

The Bourbon foster carers are called Leanne and Simon. They live in a bungalow made of brick (not biscuits), their front garden is uber-neat, and their house smells of baby wipes and tuna pasta bake. Well, it did until we turned up with our whiffy items, which immediately took over.

Haddie Baddie Boo-Boo was snoozing when we arrived so, unfortunately, I was banned from greeting her with a huge kiss and cuddle. Mum S has such a LOUD voice when she's excited, however, that I didn't have to wait long.

WOULD YOU MIND WHISPERING?
SHE'S BEEN UP ALL NIGHT.

I can confirm Haddie's SO CUTE in real life,
even when she's crying — which she does A
LOT, like when she's hungry, if she has wind
or if you wake her from a deep sleep with a
tickle under the chin . . .

When everyone had calmed down (Mums cried a
lot too — I suspect in joy as opposed to because
they also needed a poo), I held Haddie for a bit
and even gave her a bottle. She only
drinks milk at the moment. She isn't
allowed any solid food, not even a crumb
of biscuit. Harsh.

After that, we spent ages just gawping at Haddie and saying 'Oh, how adorable!' every time she moved her eyebrow or lifted her little finger. Next, Mrs Leanne Bourbon described my sister's usual routine. Essentially this boils down to: sleeping, having milk, crying, pooing, sleeping, playing, crying, having milk, sleeping, pooing, playing, bathing, crying and sleeping.

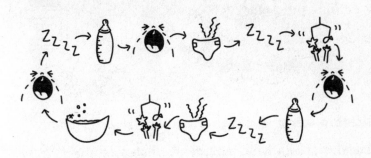

Mr Simon Bourbon mostly kept out of our way, saying he was going 'in the den'. When Haddie filled her nappy with an insane amount of sloppy poo that ponged of rotten eggs, I went to see this den. It was not a den at all. It was a small living room crammed with bookshelves, a couple of raggedy chairs and an ironing board. On the positive side, an orange-scented candle masked the poo stench so the room wasn't completely without den-building inspiration.

After a while of singing nursery rhymes and looking through an album of photos of the children the Bourbons have fostered over the years, Margaret Mulvaney turned up with Ratbag-Ruth. (Some of you might remember **her** from my second **un**SAD Diary — she's my birth mother's social worker.) A few minutes after that, a man called Solomon knocked on the door. He's Haddie's social worker. That was a lot of

people in one small living room, so I suggested
we pack up Haddie and her belongings and leave
them to have their social-worky chat.

All the adults laughed, even Mums.

'Err, Billie,' said Solomon, glancing at Mums
with raised eyebrows. 'You know you can't take
Hadbury home today, don't you?'

OMG. Listen to this utterly infuriating nugget
of information Mums insisted they'd explained
on Wednesday (possibly when I was whooping):

Haddie isn't allowed to come home and live with us forever until the solemn man thinks she is happy in our company, and Mums know all her routines inside out. He said LINKING might take 'a week or so'!

ARGH!

Even though I kind of get it, I sulked all the way home. Well, not only is it show week next week, which means I'll be extremely busy, I just want to bring my sister home so I can teach her stuff and snuggle up with her, and take her in for show-and-tell (and get her to preoccupy Mums so I can watch more TV).

DOUBLE-DARES

The Bourbons rarely have their TV on, they
NEVER have biscuits (not even Bourbons) and
TBCH looking at a sleeping baby is only fun for
two minutes maximum.

Today we had to get there by 6 a.m. just so we
could be present when Haddie woke up!

She slept in until nine . . .

Thankfully, Mr Simon Bourbon, who was as bored
as me, agreed to play Double-Dares while Mums
chatted with Mrs Leanne Bourbon about formula

(which, BTW, is not at all as interesting as it sounds — it's just what adults call powdered baby milk you have to mix with hot water).

FORMULA

NOT AT ALL MAGIC

Mr Simon Bourbon is actually quite funny. He didn't even back out when I double-dared him to put a tea towel on his head, run out on to his front lawn and shout 'NIPPLE' at the top of his voice!

NIPPLE!

When Haddie woke up, I took every opportunity to LINK with her until we had to go home.

199

We had a lovely video call with the Seasiders this evening. They're really looking forward to watching *Chiffchaff's New Gaff* (and seeing Great-Nan, of course). I've just realized that on Thursday night — our final performance — I'm going to have a FULL ROW of supporters: Mums, Granny P, Great-Nan, Raymond and the four Seasiders — Kathleen, Valerie, Robert and Toby! I'll 100% get the biggest cheer of the night.

If only Haddie could come too, my life would be complete.

PS NEVER accept a dare to taste baby formula.

EXTRA DUTIES

I got up ridiculously early
this morning to make a book
filled with photos of myself. I
gave Mums strict instructions
to hold it in front of Haddie's
face at least once every ten

minutes so she doesn't forget me. Well, Mums
are going to be LINKING with her tons more than
me this week, what with me having to go to
school and it being **SHOW WEEK** and everything.

I say 'week' but actually we're only performing
Chiffchaff three times, which doesn't seem much
considering the effort we've gone to and how
UTTERLY FANTASTIC it is. Still, I can't wait for
our opening night tomorrow. I don't think
Mrs Patterson can either. We've all
been a bit hyperactive today.

IF ONE MORE PERSON LEAVES THEIR CHAIR
TO DO A BIRD DANCE, I WILL NOT BE
HELD ACCOUNTABLE FOR MY ACTIONS!

I was possibly more excited than anyone else because I was finally able to show Class Five a photo of my sister. Most people cooed — even Mrs Patterson. Layla said she looked like me. Janey followed this by saying, 'Yes, she's beautiful!' which made my throat tighten and my eyes water. Perry said he loved my sister's pink babygrow. Dale was sweet. He revealed that, since discovering my news, he's been scouring the pavements for dropped pennies on his walks home from school so he can buy my sister a present. (He's saved up £1.10, which means he can buy Haddie anything at all from Poundworld AND afford a bag to put it in as well.) His eye has recovered, BTW. In fact,

no one was off sick today, so it looks like I won't be understudying any part.

I'm glad, TBH. Being the turkey has honestly turned out

much better than I anticipated. As part of my narrator duties, Mr Castle has asked me to deliver a 'thank you for coming' speech at the end AND to call the winning raffle tickets.

Anyway, Mr Castle made us all promise we'd get a good night's sleep before our world premiere tomorrow, so I'm going to have to go. Well, it's already nine o'clock and my 'thank you for coming' speech won't write itself. I reckon I'll be able to pen at least two pages before Mums come upstairs. Who knows, I might be able to include a song or dance . . . or two?

OPENING NIGHT!

I've just returned from the world premiere of
Chiffchaff's New Gaff. It was **AWESOME**.

Some people were terribly anxious. I wasn't,
though. Which I'm particularly glad about as
Mr Castle's advice to Layla, who
was a nervous wreck five minutes
before 'curtain-up' (aka the start
of our show, which doesn't actually
have a curtain),
was to:

PICTURE THE
AUDIENCE NAKED.

I think he thought it might make her laugh (or
calm her down), but imagining Mr Epping with
his dangly bits on show was not a pleasant
thought . . .

"SHUDDER"

The hall was **PACKED** and, thankfully, everything went a hundred times better than dress rehearsal. Most people remembered their lines and dance moves, no one was sick or blinded, and the audience laughed in all the right places.

Not only was I word-perfect, I even managed to squeeze a couple of 'ad libs' into my part. That means I cleverly made up interesting lines to keep things moving whenever anyone forgot their words. Like when Janey completely blanked (and turned a bit green) during her scene with Patrick. At which point I waited a few seconds (in case it was one of her purposeful dramatic pauses) then shot to my feet and said, 'Oh dear, Daredevil Dove doesn't look well. Perhaps she's caught a gammy-leg disease from the pigeon.' And when Farida's puffin belly popped open, causing her to get completely flustered, I marched over to her, pushed the stuffing back in and said:

NOT NOW, FIN! IT'S FAR TOO
EARLY FOR YOUR SIXTH PUFFLING
TO BE BORN!

At the end, Mums said they thought it was
wonderful and can't wait to watch it again on
Thursday with Great-Nan and the rest of the
family. According to Mum K, I am the best-
looking, best-singing, best-dancing turkey
narrator she's ever had the pleasure to call her
daughter! Hmm. I hope Haddie realizes what
she's letting herself in for.

Mrs Patterson came 'backstage' (aka into Class

One — our makeshift dressing room) after the show. She was beaming. She's so proud of the Class Five actors, set painters, mask makers and prop providers that we're allowed a TOY MORNING tomorrow!!

I've already packed my bag. I'm taking:

1. my pink tiara (for Perry — according to Peace, their dad has meanly banned him from dressing up as a princess at home)

2. my baby doll that wees when you pour water in its mouth (for Janey — to curb her insane jealousy about me and Layla both having baby sisters)

3. a pack of 'Famous Castles' Top Trumps Raymond gave me at the special home last week (mainly for Mr Castle who, despite his last name, struggles to answer

any of Elliot's castle-based
questions)

and

4. my fantabulous new 'Biscuit
Shop' that until an hour ago was a play
post office (and which, if I'm extra careful
about who I sit next to, Mrs Patterson will
never know now has a stamp drawer full of
Bourbons and a money till rammed with
custard creams).

PS Mums said Haddie's favourite thing to do
today was chew the book I made her. I can't
wait to see her again tomorrow (and rescue my
masterpiece).

MATINEE
(AKA AFTERNOON PERFORMANCE)

Our second performance of *Chiffchaff* went even better than our first. I think it was because we'd all had such a relaxing morning playing with toys, but it could also have been because Elliot and Perry swapped tights. I don't know why but, with him wearing pink tights, Perry's performance of 'Who Am I?' was the best I've ever seen him do it.

At the end, his dad gave him a gorgeous bouquet of pink roses and they had a massive hug. I'll be speaking to Mums about this at breakfast. I mean, I'm not particularly bothered about getting a bunch of 'you were marvellous, darling' flowers, but a packet of 'well done' Bourbons wouldn't go amiss.

Janey McVey's mum, dad and dad's boyfriend, Benjamin, were in the front row. They roared with laughter at the funny bits — especially Benjamin who, like me, obviously appreciates a **sp**unny **f**oonerism (!).

There were only three people specifically watching me this afternoon: Grandma Jude, Grandpa (the HOME-N-GARDEN lover) and my dear old friend Gracie Seagull, who said I was 'sensational' and the whole show was 'a spectacle to behold'. (If you don't know who Gracie Seagull is, BTW, you're just going to have to wonder. Or, better still, read my second diary — she's awesomeness personified.)

WHAT, NO SEAGULLS?!

After school I went over to the Bourbon house
with Mums. When I'd given Haddie a gazillion
cuddles, I taught Mr Simon Bourbon a few new
games he could try with my sister so she's
prepared for her move to our fun house. I'm
not sure when Haddie will be ready to play Two
Truths and a Lie, but I enjoyed catching Mr
Simon Bourbon out every time.

1. I HAVE BEEN ON TV.
2. THE PRIME MINISTER IS MY
   PEN PAL.
3. I'M WEARING PINK KNICKERS.

ERR, THE PRIME
MINISTER THING?

Plus, from the way she kicked Mrs Leanne
Bourbon in the nose after her twenty-ninth
'game' of Peekaboo, I suspect my sister's
activity preferences are similar to mine.

Anyway, tomorrow is our final (and, let's face it, my most important) *Chiffchaff* performance, so I'm going to sign off now. Not only am I super-exhausted, I need to make a couple of adjustments to my thank-you speech so it includes a special mention to the Seasiders, thanking them for journeying up the country to see me.

EMPTY . . .

When I got home from school today, Mum said she'd received a phone call from the special home informing her Great-Nan was so poorly they wouldn't be able to authorize her coming to school to watch *Chiffchaff*. 'Kathleen's not going to come either,' said Mum. 'She wants to stay by her sister's side while she can.'

Obviously I was worried about Great-Nan (and gutted she'd miss my performance), but I figured staying in the special home where nurses would keep a close eye on her was perhaps for the best.

And I totally understood how Kathleen felt. I watched Haddie play with Noodle Von Wooferson for a full

twenty-three minutes at the Bourbon house yesterday because I love her so much (not because I was keeping an extra-close eye on her dribble).

Anyway, after tea, Mums dropped me back at school. 'Try not to worry about Great-Nan,' they said before dashing off to collect Granny P. 'We'll pop over with a bottle of Lucozade tomorrow. That'll perk her up.'

I stopped worrying when Dale bounded into school. His grandad had sent him with a box of pre-performance Jaffa Cakes to share in celebration of our show's success.

By 'curtain-up' I'd cheered up completely. I walked on to the stage, my head held high, eager to impress the rest of my family, opened my mouth to begin my first bit of narration, then made the mistake of looking into the audience. Where my **crowd** of final-night supporters should have been, sat a whole **EMPTY** row of chairs.

My legs started to shake. All I could think was if Mums, Granny P, Raymond, Valerie, Robert and Toby had not made it to watch me either, something terrible must have happened to Great-Nan. I got my words messed up, fell off stage

during the Owls' Parliament dance and cried
when I sang 'Happily Ever After'.

By the time Mums arrived to take me home,
I'd prepared myself for the worst.

Just a minute. I think they're on their way
upstairs to see how I'm feeling.

CHILLI PEPPER

Sorry about that short interval. I
don't know about you, but it was a
good break for me. Mums brought
me a hot chocolate and let me drink
it in bed while we had a chat about Great-Nan.

Don't worry, BTW, 'the worst' hasn't happened —
phew. I'm not sure I'd be able to write a thing
if Great-Nan had died. The actual reason NO ONE
came to watch me tonight was this chain of
events:

1. When Mums went to collect Granny P to bring
   her to school, she'd just got off the phone
   with Valerie-the-Seasider.
   According to Granny, Valerie
   was 'extremely concerned'
   about Great-Nan.

   SHE'S GOT A VERY HIGH TEMPERATURE
   BUT SHE'S REFUSING TO LET THE
   NURSES GIVE HER ANY MEDICINE.

2. Granny P really didn't want to miss my show, but felt so worried about her mum (aka Great-Nan) that she asked Mums if they'd drop her at the special home instead.

3. Mums agreed but, when they arrived, they spotted Barmy Raymond at Great-Nan's bedroom window in floods of tears, so decided to 'nip in' to see what was going on.

4. In Great-Nan's room they were greeted by:
   a. Barmy Raymond yelling, 'It's all my

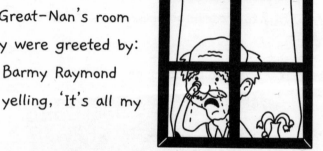

fault! I dared her to eat a red-hot chilli pepper after bingo!'

b. Great-Nan muttering swear words in her sleep, and . . .

BEEP!

c. Kathleen in a right state, wailing about how she wished she'd known decades ago about having a sister, and how much fun they could've had together singing in supermarkets and stuff.

5. The rest of the Seasiders promptly decided they couldn't leave Kathleen, as the main reason they'd come up to our village was to support her getting to know her sister, not to watch me in a show. (Hmph.)

6. By the time Mums had restored calm (and Great-Nan had woken up — phew), it was

too late for **ANYONE** to get to school to watch me.

OMG. LOOK AT THE TIME!

'We're so sorry, Billie,' said Mum S when they'd described their hectic evening again.

'We know how much you were looking forward to everyone coming to cheer you on,' added Mum K.

I **was** feeling sorry for myself. But I felt even sorrier for Great-Nan. She'd have hated everyone fussing over her when she woke up. 'Is Great-Nan honestly OK?' I asked, swigging the last of my hot chocolate.

Apparently she is, but neither of them would take me there immediately to give her a big hug. They've promised to take me straight after school tomorrow, though, so I'll be able to see for myself. According to Mums, the Seasiders are staying in a hotel again tonight, so, with any luck, I might also get to find out what Toby thinks he's found out about Zakk-O.

PS Although no one broke their leg, the applause at the end of every *Chiffchaff* performance was THUNDEROUS.

OMG!

You **WON'T BELIEVE** the day I've had.

I mean, it didn't start off terribly well . . .

I BET YOUR FAMILIES ARE IMMENSELY PROUD OF YOU!

Crying in assembly
is never a good look.

But afterwards, when Mr Castle was trying to
think of ways to make me feel better about my
disastrous final performance, and cheer me up
about Great-Nan and Kathleen missing their
first-ever sisterly theatre outing, guess who
came up with the best idea I've heard in my
whole life . . .

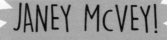

JANEY McVEY!

'Why don't we take *Chiffchaff's New Gaff* to Billie's great-nan's special home this afternoon?' she suggested.

Mr Castle exclaimed, 'What an excellent idea!' and then Janey added, 'You can play the dove if you want, Billie!'

YOU'RE LYING.

I couldn't believe my ears.

OMG! It's like Janey's had a personality transplant. She's constantly thinking about other people and how to make them happy. I stopped crying immediately, threw my arms round the pair of them and crossed my fingers it might happen.

AND IT DID!

After a lot of darting up and down the corridors, ringing everyone's parents and arguing with

Mr Epping, Mr Castle had ordered a coach, arranged everything with the special home, and straight after dinner we set off, more excited than we'd been for any of the other performances!

We had to scale things back a little as the max-volume TV room isn't as big as our school hall. I didn't mind a bit, because as soon as I walked into the performance area to sing 'The Nosedive Jive' (yes, in the knicker outfit!) I spotted Great-Nan holding hands with Kathleen and Raymond like she was the happiest woman on earth.

The whole first half went PERFECTLY. Janey was brilliant at being the turkey, Dale's breakdancing went down a storm with the old folk, Layla sang

so beautifully that one of the special-home
nurses had tears streaming down his face, and
even Patrick remembered all his lines for the
first time.

But the second half . . .

. . . WAS EVEN BETTER!

Perry was singing Chiffchaff's sweet celebration
song 'Home at Last' when Layla turned to me,
pointed to the corner of the room and whispered,
'Who's that with your mums?'

That's when I spotted Margaret
Mulvaney. I was just wondering
why Mums had brought our
ASSESSMENT social worker to
watch my play, when Mum K caught my eye and
pointed towards her feet. There between her
legs sat a purple car seat. And in the car seat,

waving her chubby little arms
around almost in time
to the music, lay MY BABY
SISTER!

'It's HADDIE!' I semi-
whispered, beaming at my sister's podgy face.

After 'Happily Ever After' and all the bowing and
cheering, I was about to run over to Mums to
find out what was going on, when the special-
home cook announced she'd organized a surprise
raffle for us as a thank you for giving the old
folk such an extraordinary treat.

'Everyone's names are inside
this pan,' she said, plunging
in her hand. 'And one lucky person is about to
win a special prize, which will be awarded to you
by one of our regular visitors — a young man I
think many of you will recognize.'

When Layla's name was pulled out, I joined in with the clapping before turning my attention back to Haddie. She looked like she'd fallen asleep. I almost requested everyone stop whooping until I realized **why** they were getting so excited.

You'll NEVER guess who was walking towards the (fake) stage . . .

ZAKK-O!

He bounded up to Layla, gave her three tickets to his next concert, told her how much he'd enjoyed her silkie-hen lament, then turned to me and said, 'Haven't we met before?'

OMG! Not only did he remember me, he knew tons of stuff about me because . . .

HE'S Barmy Raymond's great-nephew and his real name is CYRIL!!!!!!!!

THAT'S the ASTONISHING news Toby had wanted
to tell me. He was right — my
face was worth waiting for!

Before we got back on the
coach, Mr Castle gave everyone
ten minutes to chat to the old
folk. Most people declined this
opportunity in favour of crowding round 'Cyril'.
I went over to Mums who'd gone to sit with
Great-Nan. 'Is she finally ours?' I asked,
crouching beside my sister.

Great-Nan's eyes welled
with tears. 'I'm so happy,
Billie,' she said. 'Your mums
have said I can be the one
to tell you this because you
are the shining star who
brought **my** sister into
my life . . .'

YOUR SISTER IS COMING
HOME FOREVER TODAY.
CHERISH EVERY MOMENT
WITH HER.

I threw my arms round Great-Nan and we held each other for a few minutes while Mums explained what had happened. Apparently when Mr Castle had called them to tell them about our extraordinary special-home performance, they were in the middle of a meeting with Margaret Mulvaney who'd just informed them Haddie could come home FOREVER.

The timing couldn't have been more perfect. Parading my sister around for everyone to see was MILES better than doing a show-and-tell about her.

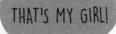

THAT'S MY GIRL!

The best news is that, by the time we were leaving the special home, Great-Nan's eyes were brighter and her skin was pink again. She said seeing me perform and meeting her new great-granddaughter had been like doses of magic medicine, and that with Kathleen by her side she felt complete.

HAPPY SISTER-GETTERS

Anyway, I'm going to have to go now. It's been a full-on few days and I'm ready for a good night's sleep.

Zzzzzzz . . .

SLEEPLESS

OMG. It's 3 a.m. and my sister has been pooing and crying on and off since midnight. I've tried to help, but even singing 'Home at Last' (from a nose-safe distance) hasn't worked. Mums are still in there now. I hope this is not going to be a regular occurrence.

Anyway, as I can't get to sleep, I thought I'd mention a couple of things I was too tired to write earlier:

1. Layla has promised me that I can have one of her spare Zakk-O concert tickets! I know it's ages off yet, but I've never been to an actual pop concert in my life. (Unless you include a Disney singalong I went to when I was about three . . . which I don't.)

2. I've suggested to Mums that a good 'well done you were an amazing turkey/dove' present might be a new SPELLINGS jotter. I really, really, really, willy, willy hope they agree because I'm pretty sure I've just overheard them discussing us driving down to Something-by-the-Sea soon. A road trip with Haddie AND a pop concert! I'm 100% going to need another STAY-AWAKE DOODLE DIARY!

TTFN! Billie X

PS Don't forget to say THRANIMAL as often as you can for the next few weeks. You never know what you could be a part of!

CHALLENGE!

Invent a new thranimal!

HOW TO PLAY
WATER–BOTTLE BINGO

(An awesome game to play during morning lessons)

1. On bits of card, draw pictures to represent all the water bottles in your classroom: one picture on each card. (You can make these as fancy or boring as you like, depending on how much time you have.)

2. Without peeking, you and your best friends select three or more cards at random.

3. Thump the air (silently) if you get the card of that kid in your class who drinks more water than a marathon runner.

4. Hide your cards somewhere so your teacher doesn't suspect you're up to something.

5. Keep your eyes on your classmates' water bottles at all times!

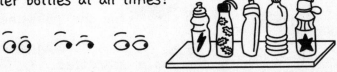

6. Turn over your card, so it's picture-side down, if the owner of that water bottle has a drink.

The WINNER is the first to turn over all (or most) cards by lunchtime.

PRIZE: exchange one lunchtime item of your choice with each loser.

 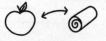

ANSWER THE QUESTION BEFORE

Remember: do not answer question 1. For all other questions, give your answer to the question before.

A

1. Name the main character of this book.

2. Who will you dress up as next World Book Day?

3. Who's the author of this book?

4. Name someone you'd like to give £1,000,000 to?

1. Do you like chocolate?

2. Did you enjoy this book?

3. Are you human?

4. Will you buy the next
   book in the B.U.G.
   series?

SERIOUS STUFF

There are currently twelve VERY SERIOUS BISCUIT LAWS to be obeyed according to TOBLA. Digest this list thoroughly or risk certain imprisonment!

1. THE CREAM-FILLED COMMANDMENT
(for things like custard creams):
Thou shalt ALWAYS remove the top layer and scrape out the cream with thy teeth.

2. THE 'LICK IT ALL OFF' LAW
(for things like chocolate digestives):
Every last scrap of chocolate must be removed with the tongue before eating (or binning) the biscuit.

3. THE 'COMPLETELY DECONSTRUCT IT' CHARTER
(especially for Jaffa Cakes):
Thou shalt endeavour to take it apart completely, saving the sweet disc of jelly till last.

4. THE CODE OF REMOVAL
(this applies to things like Clubs):
Without fail, thou shalt nibble off as much chocolate as possible before eating the remaining biscuit.

5. THE DUNKING DEMAND
(for anything dullish like a rich tea):
Thou must always dunk it — preferably in a large mug of hot chocolate.

6. THE DISGUSTING DECREE
(for all manky biscuits):
To prevent barfage, thou shalt avoid the following biscuits at all costs: Nice biscuits (aka Nasties), fig rolls (bleurgh), gluten-free ginger nuts (yuck).

7. THE SUCKING STATUTE
(for things like Penguins):
Thou shalt bite off two diagonally opposite corners, then use thy biscuit as a straw to suck up a glass of milk.

8. THE LIMB LEGISLATION

(mainly for gingerbread people):
Thou must scoff all face and button accessories before beheading, then devouring limb by limb.

9. THE MALFORMED MUST

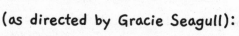

(this applies to awesomely mutant biscuits):
Thou shalt gloat gleefully, photograph the evidence and inform the newspapers before taking it to a museum for display (or enjoying it at your leisure).

10. THE VISCOUNT VERDICT

(as directed by Gracie Seagull):
Thou shalt behave like a vampire while saying, 'I vant . . . I vant . . . a Viscount!' before unwrapping and enjoying thy delicious disc of dark chocolatey-minty heaven.

11. THE 'HIDE THEM AND HOPE' AMENDMENT

(as invented by the actual prime minister):
When supplying a plate of biscuits for
meetings, one must try one's best to conceal
the tastier biscuits beneath a mountain of
dreadfully dull shortbread fingers so one can
gobble them in peace when one's guests have
departed.

12. THE PINK PROCLAMATION

(especially for pink wafers):
It is compulsory to divide pink wafers into
three distinct layers before any eating
commences.

TOBLA CHALLENGE

Billie, Dale, Layla and Janey have each invented their DREAM BISCUIT!

THICK MILK CHOCOLATE

COOKIE DOUGH

ORANGE JELLY BISCUIT

CUSTARDY CREAM

ULTIMATE COMBO

WHITE CHOCOLATE

HIDDEN MARSHMALLOW GOOP

GREEN BISCUIT

CRUMBLY CHOCOLATE BISCUIT

MOUNTAIN CLIMBER

DARK CHOCOLATE

MILK CHOCOLATE

PINK CHOCOLATE

WHITE CHOCOLATE

VANILLA CREAM

BUTTERY SHORTBREAD

SNAP 'N' SHARE

GINGER MACARONS

COCONUT SPRINKLES

PASSION FRUIT JELLY

COCONUT AND MANGO CREAM

TROPICAL SPLIT

Now it's your turn . . .

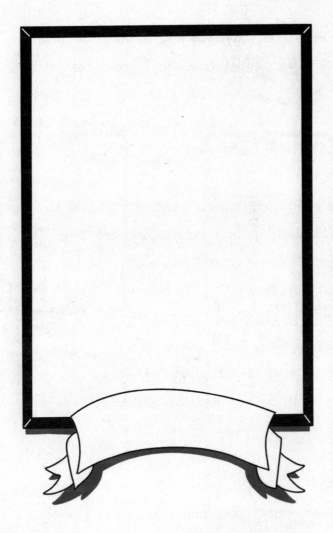

Maybe you could write a law to go with it?

SECTION $\pi\iota\sqrt{x^2}$ (ADULTS ONLY)

Good day to you, fair and intelligent grown-up person. You're looking lovely today. Have you had your hair done? Suits you.

Selecting appropriate reading material for your little darling (or class of darlings) is an EXTREMELY important job; well done for being so thoughtful. To help you out, I've developed a scientific book-picker. Don't worry, it's 100% free to participate — I know all about how adults are constantly saving up for cauliflower. (Yum, BTW.)

INSTRUCTIONS: keep your eyes on your own paper, select your category, and off you go.

Adults who are NOT teachers:	Teachers:
Pretend the child you're thinking of buying this book for is called Bernard and answer the questions below truthfully.	*Please think about the questions below and formulate your answers using fronted adverbials (always show your working).*
If you could get Bernard to eat more of something, what would it be? A. Vegetables B. Ice cream 	Are you mostly: A. kind and fun? B. mean and shouty?
What would you like Bernard to spend more time doing? A. Reading B. Watching a screen 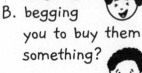	Do you like children? A. Yes B. No
Do you like it best when Bernard is . . . A. laughing? B. begging you to buy them something?	Do you enjoy buying books for the children in your class/school that . . . A. they enjoy? B. they hate?

Scientific analysis:	Scientific analysis:
Mostly As: Choose this book for Bernard. I bet you 50p he'll achieve at least two thirds of your wish list.	**Mostly As:** It would be very kind of you to buy thirty of these books so every child in your class can have a giggle while learning — it's what you do best. #BestTeacherEverOrWhat
Mostly Bs: Although Bernard sounds like he already has an amazing life, there's one thing that'd make it amazinger — this book! **PS** Please send me your contact details. I know some parents who need to learn a thing or two from you.	**Mostly Bs:** Please change jobs as soon as possible. In the meantime, please purchase thirty copies of this book for your classroom to make up for all your shouting. Thank you. Goodbye. **PS** Is that you, Mrs Patterson?

BOOK 1

BOOK 2

ACKNOWLEDGEMENTS

In addition to the remarkable team at Puffin, and the gorgeous folk at the Madeleine Milburn Literary, TV and Film Agency, I'm massively grateful to:

⭐ all the booksellers who've stocked, promoted and sold the B.U.G. series. Your support is invaluable and I hope to visit more of you in person very soon.

⭐ the wonderful librarians and inspirational teachers who promote reading for pleasure and get diverse books like mine into children's hands.

⭐ every single person who has taken the time to review a B.U.G. book online or in print. Your generous words have lifted my spirits on many an occasion.

⭐ all my readers — like YOU — thank you so much for choosing B.U.G. X

ABOUT THE AUTHOR

Jen Carney lives in Lancashire with her super-awesome family. She's passionate about representing different families in children's fiction and, like Billie, she rather enjoys dismantling biscuits.

'TWO TRUTHS AND A LIE' CHALLENGE:

1. Jen's favourite colour is green, but she dislikes green sweets.

2. Jen writes all her books in a special shed at the bottom of her garden.

3. Jen can play two recorders at the same time — using her nostrils.

Number 2 is the lie. Her shed is so small she couldn't swing a cat in it (not that cat-swinging is one of her hobbies).

HA — FOILED YOU!

This page is for all those people who have skipped ahead to see what happens in the end. All you're getting for trying to spoil the ending is this.

Now go back to wherever you were up to when this naughty idea arrived in that little head of yours (and be grateful no one's called the book police).